INTEGRATE

DISCLAIMER: This story is set in pre-2021, when local and mobile calls on public payphones in Australia were charged on a per unit basis.

Integrate

Published by Rhiza Edge, 2023
PO Box 302,
Chinchilla QLD 4413
Australia
www.wombatrhiza.com.au

Cover Layout by Carmen Dougherty.
Layout by Rhiza Press.

2nd Edition: 978-1-76111-011-5
1st Edition: 978-1-925139-09-9

A catalogue record for this book is available from the National Library of Australia

INTEGRATE

ADELE JONES

rhiza edge

In memory of Adrian Mitchell Savage
19th September 1995 - 22nd February 2012
A young man who bravely faced Mitochondrial Disease
each of his 6000 days and sparked the premise:
What if science could?

CHAPTER 1

'Don't you leave this room, Blaine Colton!'

'Whatever.' Blaine snatched his jacket from the back of his chair. As an abrupt excuse for a wave, he swiped his hand towards the woman opposite. 'Catch you at the next "science freak-boy" appointment.'

'Clearly you do *not* understand.' Dr Melissa Hartfield's eyes probed him with the sharpness of a biopsy needle. 'According to current law, *all* experimental material such as this must be contained within the facility, *particularly* GMOs. And those not approved—'

'Genetically modified organisms?' Blaine held up the jacket and backed towards the door. He wondered what had happened to the Principal Investigator that he usually liaised with for these checks. 'Not my problem, Doc. Besides, you don't own me.'

She held up a form and tapped one of the points. 'Actually, as I was explaining, technically you belong to this research institute. Not that you heard a word I said while you were browsing social media on your phone.'

Heat crept up Blaine's neck and over his face. He'd kept the iPhone near his knee and hadn't thought she'd seen it from the other side of her desk. 'Well, *I* didn't sign that form, my parents did.'

'Until you're of legal age, you can't reverse that authority without contesting it in a court of law.'

'And that's next month. Hard luck, lady. I'm out of here.'

The sound of the slamming door echoed through the corridor. Blaine's heart lurched in his chest with each stride. His new joggers squeaked their own rhythm against the impervious, laboratory-grade linoleum.

Taking his iPhone from his pocket, he started texting his mum. Hearing other footsteps much heavier than his own, he glanced over his shoulder. Two large men in security uniforms were jogging towards him.

'Mr Colton, why don't you make this easy?'

Blaine's gait stalled and he gripped his jacket tighter. They were comparative giants. Yet in his new life he had discovered himself to be wiry and fast. 'Bite me, *Baldy*.'

Having spent most of his years incapable of feeling the power of his muscles, adrenaline hit like a shot of speed. He bolted towards the exit. The corridors were strangely deserted. That worked to his advantage.

With freedom in sight, Blaine skidded to a stop as Dr Hartfield pushed through a side door and blocked his path. She held one hand behind her back. 'Blaine, I tried to explain your recent test results.'

Blaine slipped his phone into his pocket and pretended to listen, all the while inching to a better position to side-step her.

'They show the unprecedented success of your gene therapy was the result of *integration*—DNA inserting into the mutated regions of your nuclear and mitochondrial genome—not *complementation*, as stated in the approvals.'

Whatever that *means*. 'So?' He glanced over his shoulder. The security guards were walking now, but closing in.

'So? In my opinion, as this institute's Biosafety Committee

Chair, your procedure doesn't fall within the protocol approved by the appropriate regulating body. And *I'm* responsible for managing such indiscretions, including illegal GMOs.'

Again Blaine looked from her to the guards. 'I don't care about your "indiscretions". The therapy was thirty-five months ago. History! I just want to get out of here and go home.'

She shifted her hidden hand to reveal an auto-injector. Instinct kicked in. Darting nearer the wall, Blaine dropped his shoulder to barge her aside.

The collision nearly toppled him over. *But at least she's down.* He righted himself and regained his momentum.

Footsteps thudded behind him as he tore down the corridor. The guards were charging, grunting like slow, clumsy bulls. He was at the door when he felt a fistful of his shirt grabbed from behind. A huge arm reached over his shoulder, spun him around and pushed him against the wall. He struggled as Dr Hartfield strode towards him. She gripped his wrist and plunged the auto-injector towards his arm. The sting whacked him sideways. A wave of nausea coursed through his body.

He looked to his upper arm and caught a hazy glimpse of the auto-injector, now delivering its venom. His jacket slid from his arm to the floor with a plop. It was like he'd been submerged in a giant tub of honey.

Still he struggled. 'Stop! You can't do this.'

The thugs had him pinned. Dr Hartfield shook her head. 'We can, Blaine. If you'd been listening, you'd know that.' Her words grated like jarring noises through his mind. 'Blaine, *you're* the illegal GMO.'

Illegal ... GMO ... me ...?

'Take him to the observation room.'

CHAPTER 2

'You could have made this much simpler, Blaine.'

Blaine groaned. 'My head.' He squinted through heavy eyelids, just enough to catch an out-of-focus glimpse of Dr Hartfield sitting on a nearby chair. *What is this lady's sudden interest in me?*

She'd provided no explanation as to why the usual liaison, the Principal Investigator who conducted the study, hadn't been at the meeting. Once, under some special request arrangement he'd even met Professor Ramer, the developer of his therapy. Dr Hartfield was a mystery. He knew her only as Chief Scientist of Advance Research Institute, acronym ARI, and had never even *spoken* to her until that unscheduled emergency meeting he'd stormed out of.

'It's a shot and a half, but you left us little choice. We're not trying to *kill* you. Although technically, if you were *any* other species, that would be the unquestionable action required.'

Bracing with difficulty, Blaine propped himself up on his elbow. He realised he'd been laid upon a hospital-style bed. 'May as well kill me.' He felt uneasy at how slurred his voice sounded and how blurred Dr Hartfield's face looked.

Dr Hartfield sighed. 'Blaine, it's not that bad. It's just a little difficult to know what to do. I don't want the Government's regulating body involved until we understand exactly what we're dealing with.'

Blaine snorted and tentatively manoeuvred his legs over the edge of the mattress. 'Isn't that also illegal?' His eyes still refused to focus properly, but he took a quick glance about the room. To all appearances, it was identical to the one where he'd been housed while undertaking Professor Ramer's gene therapy. *Great. Back in observation.* He eyed the mirrored half-wall and pulled a face.

Running his hands down his cargo jeans, he patted his hip pockets, then the zip-ups above the knee, and then the rear pockets. 'Where's my phone? I want to ring my parents.'

'I've taken your phone for safe keeping, and your wallet.'

'You've *what*?' Blaine slid from the bed and grabbed the frame with whitened knuckles. *Stop spinning, head.* It wasn't listening. *Got to get outta here.*

'Blaine?' Dr Hartfield came to her feet in a smooth, singular motion. 'Can you walk?'

He noticed she wore a surgical gown and consistently remained beyond his reach. Testing his legs, he realised he could indeed walk. But after only a few steps his knees felt like chocolate melting in the sun. Gritting his teeth, he tottered behind her into a small, sterile-smelling alcove. He slumped down onto a metal bench.

'Not a bad view.'

Blaine lifted his head and realised they were on an enclosed balcony. He narrowed his eyes to view the cityscape. The sun had long since bowed to night and a scatter of lights glittered in a meandering curve to the distant horizon.

ARI was situated on the border of a new industrial estate in Brisbane's southwest. Attached to the institute was a hospital for routine patient care, and another unit that ran clinical trials. That was where he usually had his follow-up appointments. The industrial estate eased into residential subdivisions just a few streets away, but that suburb didn't have a high reputation. Blaine preferred not to be wandering its streets at night, so ensured he made his appointments with ample time to get home before sunset.

Not today, though.

He could feel Dr Hartfield's eyes upon him. Jaw set, he wondered how hard he'd have to push to get back his mobile phone and wallet. They provided access to *everything* important for his daily living, from social media and communication, to public transport and banking; not to mention his prized possession—his brand new learner driver's permit. 'What now?'

'We've recently discovered Professor Ramer, as lead scientist of the collaborative research group that developed your therapy, did not include some crucial details of your treatment when submitting approval requests for your trials. As such, we have to assess the risk.'

'Risk of *what*?' Blaine scowled at her and hoped the expression looked as awful as he felt.

'Viral transmission.'

'After nearly three years?'

Her eyes were bland. 'Records state you experienced a life-threatening reaction to your gene therapy, which was *supposed* to introduce short sequences of wild-type—undamaged—DNA into your cells through non-infectious virus-like particles. Those sequences were to complement, that is, counter, the mutations causing your mitochondrial disease—like a patch for a broken circuitry connection. But it appears the vector was neither "virus-like" nor avirulent. That means there is every possibility you could be carrying an uncharacterised, potentially disease-causing virus. Consider the people you've contacted in that time.'

Blaine only partially understood and wondered if she was deliberately talking down to him to make him feel inferior. Was what she had told him right? It *sounded* like it could be, but he didn't know enough to judge. That didn't stop the memories that flashed through his mind. He flinched, instantly reliving the weeks of furious fever and body pains that had racked his body. Not the best fifteenth birthday present. It had nearly killed him.

He shook off the sensation with a slight quiver. It was over now and it had certainly been worth it. 'That's research, I s'pose.'

'*Research* to the tune of a quarter of a million dollars if fined, or imprisonment, for the breach.'

Blaine felt the involuntary rise of his eyebrows. 'What about the Principal Investigator of the trial? Have you asked him? Or Professor Ramer's research team? Have you asked *any* of them about this?'

'It doesn't matter what the PI, Ramer or his team think. *All* work involving genetic manipulations in Australia must be approved by the appropriate authorities *prior* to its undertaking, *especially* something like this. That's why we've had to access your case report form against routine protocol, and also trace your activities since the procedure.'

Her incisive eyes focussed on Blaine like the halogen headlights of a sports car—*a svelte red Ferrari, in fact. With a sleek chassis ...* Admiring her streamlined design, it took a few seconds for her meaning to sink in. 'Hang on.' Blaine came unsteadily to his feet. 'You've been *stalking* me?'

'Not stalking exactly, just regulars tabs on financial transactions, telephone accounts, social media, GPS tracking and such. It's not difficult.'

'That's a breach of privacy!'

She offered a condescending smile that returned him to his seat. 'You might want to check the study agreement. Besides, after running the first block of tests we may determine there is no apparent risk and be able to have you downgraded—despite the fact you are still *technically* illegal.'

'Huh?'

'Demonstrate you're low risk.'

'How long for that?'

'I—ah—really cannot say. Maybe a few days? Maybe weeks?'

'And?'

'Well, you'll still be an unapproved GMO and may never be able to move about freely.'

'From the facility?'

Dr Hartfield shrugged an apology.

Eyes locked on the grey-flecked floor covering, Blaine slowly shook his head. 'No way. You can't do this.' He looked up into her face, his focus much clearer now. 'I *want* to call my parents. What about my friends?'

'Fine. You can call your parents, although I already have so they wouldn't worry. It wouldn't hurt to personally reassure them that you're all right.'

Dr Hartfield left him for a moment. The heels of her lab-safe shoes made a dull clomp with each step. She paused to swipe her ID card to exit the room.

Blaine didn't even have time to order his roiling thoughts before she was back. She set his iPhone on the seat beside him. The fact she was wearing latex examination gloves didn't escape his attention. *What am I? Some sort of disease?*

He glanced at her as he picked up the phone. Desperately, he tried to marshal the thoughts wrestling in his mind. *What can I say? Am I really all right?*

'Before you call, you need to consider why you're here.'

Blaine held the mobile in his hand and stared at it. The tumbling thoughts stilled. 'What do you mean?'

'Undoubtedly you want to go home, but what will that mean for your parents?'

As he looked up, she held his eye for a moment. Blaine said nothing.

'Don't you think it would be unfair to distress them further?' she persisted. 'What would it gain you, or them, to alarm them with talk of your illegal status? You could drag them into all this, risking imprisonment or fine—or worse, their health.'

Turning his attention back to his phone, Blaine let her words sink in. Certainly, they'd be worried crazy if he started gibbering about being held against his wishes and wanting them to come and get him. Irony was, that was exactly what he'd planned on doing.

The scene played out in his mind; his parents storming into Dr Hartfield's office and demanding his release, only to be carted away by security guards or the police.

Haven't they been through enough at my expense since adopting me? Near financial ruin. Emotional exhaustion. If criminal charges were added ...

With a deep breath, he held down the centre button, activating speech recognition. 'Call home.' The request repeated back to him as his parents' landline flashed up and the number dialled. The phone started ringing and was answered almost immediately.

'Hi Dad, it's Blaine.'

'Son, are you okay? Dr Hartfield said they've admitted you for additional testing—just a precaution, apparently, but I ... I don't understand. What could have changed since your recent checks? Are they looking after you? Has the PI confirmed these extra checks are in keeping with the study agreement protocol?'

9

He glanced at Dr Hartfield as his father asked this string of questions. Concern etched every query. 'Yeah, Dad, I'm fine. They just need to check a few things. And everything was good on the follow-up report. Just a couple of tests to wait on. I'll be here a few days, maybe more.'

'You remember I'm leaving the country in a couple of days?'

Blaine sucked in a breath. 'Yeah, I know you've got your conference trip this week.'

'Do you want me to cancel? I will, if you need me to.'

He frowned at his father's question. Everything in his mind screamed. *No!* He didn't want his dad to fly to the other side of the world while he was trapped like a toad pinned to a dissection tray. But he knew how long his father had waited for this opportunity.

Previously, Blaine's health had been a fragile bubble, waiting to pop in the lightest breeze. If work-related travel involved anything more than a day away from home, his dad had always passed. Their only international family trip had been for his treatment. Even now his mother couldn't be convinced to join the adventure, despite his father suggesting she should come. It had really restricted his dad's career options, until now ...

'Dad, you've been planning this for months. Go. Have fun. I'll be okay.'

'Okay, then. I love you, Blaine. And I'll be praying.'

Blaine nearly rolled his eyes. 'Yeah, I know. You too. Bye.'

The call ended and the screen returned to the front page. He stared at his wallpaper picture and smiled.

Sophie.

'Special girl?'

Blaine's head snapped up and he realised Dr Hartfield was looking over his shoulder. He shrugged and set his phone back on the bench, screen down. He figured if they'd been tracking him since his treatment, they'd know who Sophie Faraday was.

Former neighbours. *Was that all they knew? Maybe.* He hadn't seen Sophie and her twin brother, Jett, as much since their family had moved. They kept in frequent contact though, and Sophie had messaged him just a few nights ago. She'd told him about her university studies and had wanted to congratulate him on getting his learner's permit. Clearly their mothers had been talking.

'Look, Blaine, I'm sorry it has to be like this. Truly I am.'

He shrugged again, eyes back on the floor. Sophie was a fool's dream anyway.

CHAPTER 3

'Good morning, Blaine. How are we today?'

Blaine refused to acknowledge the 'white coats'. They were supposedly a team of scientific attendants but to him they were more like prison wardens. Late into the night he'd explored his room—*gotta face the truth: not a room, a holding cell*. He'd peered as far as he could through the viewing glass. There was only one way out, and it required swipe card access.

The door to his cell opened to a small anteroom. He presumed the corridor beyond it led to a lab where his treatment was developed. Maybe. His cell had an enclosed balcony to give it less of a prison feel. But it was fully secured, and he figured the window was one-way glass, like the rest of the building's exterior.

Lying flat on his back, he pretended he was again living in his atrophied body. *Perhaps if I con them into thinking I've relapsed, there'll be panic.* He had learned over his years as a silent observer that whenever there was panic there were always mistakes. *Maybe even a door could be left ajar ...*

A plan, perhaps, but it was ruined by the grumbling of his stomach as a tray of breakfast was delivered.

Maybe I'll try that tomorrow ...

After guzzling down a bottle of spring water, Blaine layered multiple slices of the best cheese he'd ever tasted with thinly-shaved shoulder ham onto warm croissants. Fresh fruit salad was accompanied by a side serve of Honey Buzz yoghurt. *My favourite. Done their homework, haven't they?*

When breakfast was over, he sat on the enclosed balcony looking out. He heard an ambulance scream towards the nearby hospital, saw a truck drive in and another out of the industrial estate, but that was all.

After only an hour he was bored beyond reason, so decided to do a short workout. The bench was a good height to use as a step for jump-ups and stretches, and for propping up his feet as extra resistance when doing push-ups. He knew the floor would be pristinely clean—more than enough for him to do sit-ups and any floor routine he wished. The only thing lacking was an overhead bar for chin-ups.

Lathered with sweat, he went into the tiny ensuite to shower. He looked at the bidet and grinned. Sure, it would be practical when catering for mobility-impaired persons, but it was weird having one in his bathroom.

He showered, dried himself and began to redress. His clothes were still damp and stank of day-old sweat. Wrapping the towel around his waist, he rinsed out his underwear and held them in the Airblade hand-dryer. They were soon dry enough to wear without chafing. He freshened up the rest of his clothing by passing them through the warm, high velocity air.

Wearing just his jeans, he exited the small alcove to find Dr Hartfield waiting for him.

'We could have laundered your clothes and given you a hospital gown instead.' Her eyes scanned his bare upper body. 'There are facilities available nearby.'

13

'I prefer to wear my own things.' Heat crept up Blaine's neck and face and then spilled out over his entire body—but it wasn't Dr Hartfield's presence triggering his reaction.

Thinking back through the past few days, he realised he had forgotten to take his meds two days running. This would be the third day without the medication essential to the maintenance of his gene therapy.

How could I be so stupid?

The occasional miss, sure, but two days in a row was entirely out of character. Three was dangerous.

Had he been so preoccupied by Sophie's message that all sense had been knocked from his head? Was he just anxious over the unscheduled follow-up assessment? They always made him a little nervous.

'You can leave your shirt off. I have to attach some electrode pads.' Dr Hartfield paused, as if awaiting a response. 'Blaine, are you all right?'

He nodded and sank down onto the chair near the bed. Sweat popped out all over his face and hands, and began to trickle down his back. His vision clouded up and he knew that a fever spike could put him over the edge. *Slow, calm breathing...* 'All right, sure ...'

A glimpse at Dr Hartfield's face proved she didn't believe him. Instead, her scrutiny increased. 'Blaine, I want to detail the next few days with you. As I mentioned, we'll need to run a few tests, which means more blood work and biopsies. I know this doesn't excite you, but it will give us a better indicator of where you're at. I'll pop these pads on now and get you hooked up for monitoring.'

Gripping the arm rests, Blaine pressed himself back in the padded seat. Everything went out of focus and Dr Hartfield's words turned to meaningless prattle. Cords were clipped to monitors and the hollow burble continued until it sounded like a loud hum.

As if taunting him in his misery, he felt the fever spike begin and a machine squealed like some tattle-tale in a primary school playground. He knew this alert would bring a multitude of attendants.

Blaine fought to remain conscious as heat razed through him. A company of white coats gathered about, suffocating his darkening view until all he could see was black dots.

'I thought the convulsions had ceased since his therapy?' He heard one of them say.

'Is he on any prescription drugs?'

'There's nothing specified in the case reports I've seen. Just some supplement.'

Blaine sensed he was approaching seizure. 'Do. Something.' But no one moved.

Why don't they know about the 'Cure'?

The silhouettes with their clipboards, monitors and piqued curiosity haloed his obscured view.

'Is this what you meant about the carrier *not* being avirulent, as Professor Ramer claimed?' one of the coated assistants remarked.

'Yes, this was my fear—that whilst repairing his mitochondrial mutations, another disease has been created. And now *he* could be genetically programmed to replicate that pathogen in his own cells.' Dr Hartfield's voice was muffled by a N95 respirator. Her voice was calm and precise as she read the display of each monitor attached to the specimen.

I'm still here, people, and I'm not *a lab rat.*

'Take every precaution until we know exactly what was used and have determined what genetic material was incorporated.'

'H-help me.' Blaine gargled, his body beginning to spasm.

'Just a little longer, Blaine. We know what your body can take before there's irreversible damage.'

Blaine wanted to curse at this unseen person, but his jaw locked. *Entering last stage… oh God, help.* His vision gone, he could only hear the voices of the coats.

'That's enough. Administer something to try and drop his temp.'

'Paracetamol i.v.?'

'*Might* work.'

'Might not—then what?'

'What about an anticonvulsant?'

Feeling like he had gone ten rounds in a professional boxing clash, Blaine lay helpless on the surgical table. The discussion of the coats swarmed through his mind like mosquitoes over swampy water.

'Wait, hold off on the meds. I'd like to find out what's causing the reaction first. I'm surprised he's managed those spikes, especially lately, with the increased frequency. It's like … well, I wouldn't like to guess. There's also nothing about post-treatment seizures on his records. Get serology, immunohistochemistry and metagenomic analysis underway.'

'Will have some results within hours, Melissa, all going well.'

'Dr Hartfield, should we try to match any sequences we acquire against the experimental strains previously held in Ramer's stocks? Isn't there a duplicate collection on site that hasn't been shipped yet—you know, the backup stocks, in case anything was lost in transit?'

A tense male voice interrupted the high-pitched, squeaky one that seemed to have a severe case of 'fangirl'.

'Those *should* have been destroyed, once the stocks were successfully transferred. Even if they weren't, we're not allowed to access those, Mel. And certainly not without written permission or—'

'*I'm* giving her permission, *Eddie*. This is an exceptional situation. I've explained this already.'

'Seriously?'

Squeaky fangirl jumped back in. 'Do you also want us to generate antibodies to screen the isolates?'

'*There* are your antibodies.' This voice was like whiplash, cracking sharp and cold in Blaine's mind. 'If it's viral, it clearly has a decent host immune evasion strategy.'

'Which should narrow down our diagnosis.' Dr Hartfield seemed to have forgotten Blaine's health episode, now reaching crisis point.

'What does it matter? It's integrated into the genome. It's not like we can jump it out.'

'But if we can devise a way to replicate the process *without* inferring the virulent attributes …'

'But obviously that vigour enabled biological distribution through his entire body—and hence was able to rectify the condition so effectively.'

'Dr Hartfield, do you think we can isolate whatever it is, without eliminating the host?' Fangirl again. The man who had challenged Dr Hartfield grunted an objection. But the words hit home.

Eliminating the host. Eliminate. Host.

Blaine tried to move; tried to remind them he was not some mouse in a cage. They talked on, discussing him as if he had no ears or brain with which to process their conversation. *Help!* His vision splintered into focus for a moment, enough to see a blonde fuzz bobbing above a N95 respirator. And that was the last thing he remembered.

Blaine had no idea how long he was out. He'd been rolled into the recovery position and Dr Hartfield was back in the chair, waiting for him with concern etched across her brow. He couldn't see her mouth. The respirator was on, and her eyes peered out from behind a thin plastic shield protecting her eyes.

Blaine turned his head to look straight at the distorting lamps above. He smelled the familiar odour of the room. *Clean—sickly so.* He fought a strong urge to throw up.

As feeling returned, he noticed something pulling at the skin of his left arm, either side of his elbow. Clumsily, he shuffled the arm, then realised it was a cotton ball secured with tape. *Vampires.*

He jiggled his head. 'Some new life *this* is.'

'I'll leave you for a while to recover. Don't worry, you'll be closely monitored and we've got medical staff on call. The hospital is only a walk away, if needed.' Dr Hartfield swiped her card and left. The door clicked heavily behind her.

With his strength returning, Blaine pushed himself to a sitting position and waited for his head to remember it wasn't a yo-yo. That had been the worst seizure he'd suffered since the gene therapy. The occasional fever spike he was used to managing, but the seizures were embarrassing.

He looked down at his jeans. They now needed proper laundering. The mirrored wall reflected his face. When he saw the eggshell hue of his sweat-lacquered skin, he groaned. His dark, wavy hair stuck to his scalp. He ruffled it up before pretending to pick his nose for the benefit of the guard sure to be watching from behind the one-way wall.

CHAPTER 4

Blaine lay on the bed in a hospital gown and stared at the ceiling. It was another morning of a seemingly eternal Groundhog Day.

Though it's probably only been two. Maybe three.

He mentally tacked a set of Post-It notes on a wall in his mind and tried to connect them.

One: I managed to get the bag of tablets from my jeans before they insisted on this hospital gown and stash it behind the toilet. One tick for hope.

Two: For some reason they've no idea about the Cure. No idea how to control my condition. They won't know how much I can fake. Two ticks for hope.

Three: So long as the fevers don't spike too badly, I won't have to use the tablets. I can save them to help me escape. Three ticks for hope.

The light blazed directly over him. Its whiteness blended into the sterile walls. If he stared at it long enough, he could close his eyes and watch the negative on the back of his eyelids. Besides the large mirrored half-wall, there was no glass in the observation room—just fishbowl-like surveillance. If it weren't for the alcove the with view, he'd be shark-in-a-goldfish-bowl stir-crazy.

Four: Given my medical history, they'd never guess how good my hearing is. Supersonic, Dad calls it. Or my sense of smell. And they discuss everything in front of me as if I'm mentally impaired.

He remembered the times his mother had tried to redirect the talk in front of his wheelchair by people who assumed he had zero IQ. In the main her efforts had been futile, and he'd received quite an education. Some days his thoughts had been more like dreams, as if his brain couldn't be bothered operating fully conscious. But the information still went in, filed for later reference.

Blaine had a theory about this ability. He had a mitochondrial disorder and mitochondria were the powerhouses of the cell. If they weren't working properly, it made sense that the body had to conserve energy where it could. Instead of shutting down completely, he felt like his brain went into 'standby mode'. But even post-therapy, as if born of habit, his mind still subconsciously absorbed enormous quantities of information and then regurgitated it later for 'processing'. Even when he was practically asleep. It was bizarre, but certainly an advantage when planning his escape.

He closed his eyes, inhaled deeply and listened. He could hear faint sounds from some equipment nearby. Familiar sounds. He tried to identify them.

Dad's work … Blaine's dad was his company's hygienist and there was a quality assurance lab near his office. Many times during the pre-gene therapy years, Blaine's wheelchair had been parked in the corner of his father's office. He'd grown accustomed to those distant laboratory sounds—sounds just like the ones he was hearing now.

Even while undergoing intense post-treatment rehabilitation, Blaine had occasionally gone with his dad on school holidays. Assisted by a walker, he'd eventually gotten to *see* the lab. Well, from the door, where his father pointed out different staff members and equipment.

He'd never admit it to his friends, but it had been kind of cool hanging out at his dad's work. And the surprise visits mum would delight in, because she couldn't wait to show off each quantum miracle as, one by one, his speech, mobility and general bodily function normalised.

But Dad had surprised them both the day Blaine ditched the walking frame and toddled into a run for the first time. Having secretly enlisted the neighbours, being Sophie and Jett's family, they'd arrived home to find the house spilling over with people and the lounge room so full of balloons they were drifting out the door and down the hall. His wheelchair was on display with a huge 'For Sale' sign on it. The party went on for hours. Every time he popped a balloon, someone gave him a gift. It was wild.

Blaine felt tears forming in his eyes. Even though a part of him cringed each time his mother retold the story, he understood his parents' excitement. At the time it'd been one of the best days of his life. But seriously? He'd been sixteen. What sixteen-year-old does stuff like that? *But what sixteen-year-old defies a genetic death sentence and lives to tell the tale?*

A very blessed one.

His parents said stuff like that to him every day. Blaine hammered the back of his head against his pillow, as if this action could knock the words from his head. He was always blessed. Always a gift from God. Just like they were always praying.

He didn't resent his parents' faith, he just wasn't sure where he fit with it, or it with him. In reality his life had never been his own to decide. He believed there was something. A spiritual realm. God. But had never had the option of exploring it for himself, until recently. To test it. Prove it. *And how would I do that anyway?* He frowned at the ceiling.

Re-focus. He had to learn more about the facility and work out a plan. Concentrating on his surroundings, he heard a gusty drone rise above the constant hum. *Possibly a fume cupboard? Definitely something with fans.*

A sudden tink sounded even closer. *Glassware. Could the lab be on the other side of the wall?* In all his time spent in post-treatment observation, he'd never been anywhere near a lab.

Blaine smiled. Lab thoughts reminded him of when he'd been caught hacking into his father's digital scientific journal subscriptions. He'd merely wanted to understand his condition and treatment more thoroughly, but he'd never seen his father's eyes as wide as when he'd realised what his son had done. This devious use of intellect had seemed more of a shock than his parents could handle.

Rather than a reprimand, Blaine had been encouraged to enrol in online courses and take extra-curricular science activities through school. It didn't hurt that Sophie had been mad set on doing science at university and had eagerly explored the world of gene therapy with him. Until she left ...

Wait, that's five ticks! I know a heap more than they think I do.

His nose twitched. A new smell. *Was it coming through the air ducts?* The faint fragrance was a slight alleviation to the pervasive sterility. Blaine sniffed at the initial fruity-citrus top notes and tried to identify the heart and base. Adept at 'perfume speak', he knew it would be easy.

His mother, a Le Rêve representative, often trialled the products at home before hosting a party. Blaine had been her captive audience over the years. Fruity, floral, oriental, woody—he could nearly detect the notes as well as a sniffer dog.

Another deep breath perfused his lungs with mid-note geranium and vanilla, under which swelled a rich base with woody undertones ... He inhaled again. *Patchouli?* It was all he could do to stop the tear that dotted the corner of his eye. He was certain he could smell his mother's signature perfume.

Wishful thinking. The tear slid down his face, but he crushed it into his skin with his palm. He was nearly eighteen, not a cry-baby pre-schooler

His brow creased and he turned his nose towards the door. He was puzzled as the aroma grew stronger. Moments later Melissa Hartfield opened the anteroom door, lab coat, gloves, respirator and face shield in place.

She's wearing Mum's signature.

CHAPTER 5

'I need to call my parents. *Now.*'

Melissa eyed Blaine through the plastic visor. She had known this would come. Careful not to demonstrate undue emotion and thus catalyse his own reactions, she handed back his clothes—decontaminated, laundered and dried—and considered the best way to negotiate the matter.

'Blaine, if you call again it will only concern them more. Besides, do you *really* want them caught up in all of this? Didn't you say your dad was leaving today for his first international conference in years?' She watched him closely, waiting for him to detect her sincerity. 'You know, Blaine, they've dealt with a lot through the years.'

Melissa had seen the extensive list of natural and pharmacological remedies and procedures the Coltons had trialled over time. Though none were highly effective, all were costly. They believed that long term this saved Blaine's vital organs and central nervous system from permanent damage. She reserved her opinion. Yet she understood these treatments, along with the life-saving care and devices they had acquired on his behalf, had forced them to make some harsh financial decisions. But finance was just the start—and Blaine knew it. She paused to let the facts sink in and saw his eyes cloud.

She seized on this sign of vulnerability. 'Have they ever spoken about how they felt when you were diagnosed? All that hope of rescuing a needy child, only to discover your life expectancy was less than ten years.'

Blaine's eyes shot up and locked on her face. They were dark, accusing.

'That's a lie! My parents knew. They adopted me to help *save* my life.'

She took a long breath and shook her head. 'Blaine, I'm sorry. I thought they would have told you. I suppose it must have been a shock, and then to carry the burden of your care into your teens ... I understand them wanting to explore every treatment option within their means.'

'They said I was a gift—special, just for them.'

She watched him flush, as if he realised the childishness of his words. 'They may have felt that, but I'm telling the truth. You can *trust* me. I have a copy of your medical records. It's there in black and white. Your condition *wasn't* diagnosed until *after* your adoption.' She softened her tone. 'It must have been a challenging commitment for them.'

Blaine fixed his focus on the end of his bed. 'Can't I let them know I'm still all right?' He glanced up, his brown eyes dulled with uncertainty.

Melissa smiled but Blaine didn't respond. She realised belatedly he wouldn't be able to see her mouth. 'Of course. I'll call them again.'

'Why can't I speak to them?'

She shook her head and tried to emanate sympathy. 'I'm sorry, Blaine. It would only complicate things more if you gave them another reason to worry.'

'And they won't now?'

'I've told them you've had to have more tests, that it's nothing to worry about and you'll be home in a week, or so.'

Blaine's eyes darted up like two beacons blazing with hope. 'A week? Really?'

'We'll see. But Blaine,' she held his gaze, '… you must know I've got your best interests in mind. I don't want you to be hurt. I want to protect you. That's why you must stay here until we can sort things out with the regulating body. And that's why I wouldn't lie to you about your diagnosis.'

His shoulders hunched as he nodded. Melissa watched him for a moment more before swiping her ID card at the door and leaving.

The door had scarcely closed when Blaine heard a colleague call Melissa from the other side of the anteroom. Even when she had decontaminated and passed on through, their voices were clear.

'Dr Harfield, his serology lights up with *everything*.' It was one of the coats.

'Everything?'

'Well … we've recorded cross-reactions with *all* the vector-suitable isolates cultured from Ramer's duplicate stocks, thus far.'

For the benefit of surveillance, Blaine feigned disinterest. Best to let them think a nearly eighteen-year-old rehabilitated vegetable knows nothing about immune responses and genetic engineering.

Turning onto his side, he honed every auditory sensor on the voices at the door. Dr Hartfield sounded sceptical. 'And in just a few days you've been able to test *all* those isolates?'

'Well … no … three, but his biochemistry's a bit odd. Do you think that could be part of it?'

'Did you report any toxic metabolites? And the reality is, Blaine's biochemistry will always be inconsistent until the treatment is properly regulated. Even then, it's unlikely to ever be "normal". What about the metagenomic analysis?'

There was a long pause. Blaine waited for the colleague's reply, but they'd started moving away, for the man's next words were barely perceivable.

It cross-reacts with 'everything'?

Blaine ran through the viruses he had previously considered might have been genetically modified to deliver his treatment. Adeno-associated virus and couple of tropical disease pathogens were top of his list, but he knew even HIV had been utilised for gene modifying applications. Yet, if this was the reason for his lingering symptoms, nothing he'd looked into *quite* matched.

If he was understanding Dr Hartfield correctly, he now knew why.

Professor Ramer must have engineered the viral vector from multiple microorganisms.

He stopped.

Perhaps he was wrong. If not, had the Professor and his group handpicked the sequences they wanted and pieced them together, creating a new, dangerous organism for use as a delivery vector? *And now that those sequences have integrated into my genome … ?*

For the first time since his treatment, Blaine felt a claw of fear. He knew that when DNA was joined together, given the right sequence combinations, previously repressed genes could be activated, or even non-existent open reading frames unintentionally created.

Previously repressed genes were one thing, but an entirely *new* sequence could produce *anything*. *What if the persistent fevers are from a toxin being expressed? What if that toxin slowly builds up in my system until I can't manage it any longer, unless I take my medication?*

The hook of fear pierced deeper. *What if Professor Ramer invented a new disease and, through me, released it to the world?*

Surely, he did animal trials and wouldn't have infected a human host if he wasn't confident of the outcome. But what if he didn't ...?

No wonder they've got me here. I'm a walking biohazard!

Dr Hartfield's comment about unauthorised GMOs dripped through Blaine's head.

If I were any other species, I would have been destroyed without question. That's what she said.

Doubt crowded his mind as her remarks regarding his adoption tapped at his heart.

He'd been told his condition had first been diagnosed as a ten month old. His birth mother had been advised he should be 'terminated'. Of course, the more politically correct term was DNR, 'do not resuscitate'. Even euthanasia had been hinted at, unofficially, or so he'd been told. Essentially the directive was to let nature take its course—with a little bit of help from the medical profession.

But was that the truth? Had his parents selflessly intervened? Or were they victims of cruel fate, thinking they were getting an unwanted baby with several simple developmental delays due to a temporary health problem?

Blaine's parents had told him they'd been on the adoption waiting list for years, undergoing all manner of assessments. By coincidence, or divine destiny as they claimed, they'd been called to the same hospital where he was in care and were told of his plight. They applied to adopt him under the special needs category and were eventually approved.

It had always been beyond his comprehension as to why they'd picked him with all his disabilities. They talked about heaven's choice for them—sang him songs of hope and saving grace. He'd never been wholly convinced.

Was Melissa Hartfield right?

With a twist of a knife in his heart, he remembered the diamond pattern on the leggings of the woman who stood in front of his wheelchair and berated his mother for wasting her public resources on a child that nature had destined to die. *And the stone-washed jeans of the man who spat at …* He corralled the bleak memories and sent them away. Only the present question mattered.

Did Mum and Dad lie to protect me—or themselves? Have they lied about anything else?

These thoughts struck a wound deep in his heart.

The gene therapy had changed his life. The clinical trial information package on the treatment developed by Professor Ramer's group had never claimed anything other than a radical, aggressive approach. Blaine had nothing to lose.

Now I've got everything to lose. I'm an illegal, potentially infectious GMO. I'm faced with the same threat as when I was a baby. Unless I can be 'downgraded'.

Blaine rolled onto his back and ground his knuckles against his eyes. He appraised the health history of his friends and family. No one had become infected through him.

Then again, what if the created virus required an insect host for transmission, like the right fly or mosquito? If it *was* virulent and only required the right insect to bite him—then what?

The insurmountable reality of his status as an unauthorised GMO crushed down on him like a giant, pounding wave. 'Mum, Dad …' His voice broke as he swallowed back tears. 'Please come, no matter what they say. Please come get me.'

But what if they don't want me anymore?

The thought of living out his few remaining days in this blindingly white fish tank made him even more determined to escape. He flipped over onto his stomach and thumped his fist against the pillow.

CHAPTER 6

'Good morning, Dr Hartfield speaking.' Melissa glanced across the desk at her colleague, Dr Edward Jonick, knowing he was listening closely to her conversation.

'Dr Hartfield, it's Belinda Colton—*again*. What's happening with our son? Your executive assistant assures me you're the appropriate person to provide this information, but you keep dismissing my enquiries. Where is the Principal Investigator of Blaine's study? I cannot get onto him.'

'Mrs Colton, I explained this previously. The Principal Investigator is unavailable—on leave actually, for a month. We've had to send Blaine for a few more tests, as some results from his recent follow-up appointment were inconclusive. But it's nothing to worry about.'

'Nothing to worry about? Blaine has a serious health condition that requires careful monitoring, even given his gene therapy. As he's not yet eighteen, he's our responsibility. This is *completely* outside the conditions of his clinical trial, which were communicated when we signed the consent agreement. My husband and I have a *right* to know the specifics of your investigation.'

She rolled her eyes at her colleague. *Not again*, she mouthed. 'Yes, I understand your concerns, Mrs Colton. I know it's been six days. But he's fine.'

'Why can't I reach him on his phone?'

'He can't have it on. It interferes with the equipment. The tests are merely precautionary.'

'And you're managing the fevers? If his condition's unmanaged, he can also experience seizures.'

'We know about his fevers and seizures.'

'And he's got enough meds? The ones developed by Professor Ramer's research group? It's a part of the treatment maintenance.'

She stopped and pressed the handset harder to her ear. 'Medicine from Professor Ramer?' Eddie leaned forward; his eyes locked on hers.

'Yes. Blaine was supplied the tablets with strict administration instructions via the Principal Investigator.'

Melissa scowled, finding it hard to follow the woman's emotional prattle, let alone decipher cryptic remarks about undocumented medication. 'It's *not* prescription?'

'I just said that. You *do* know what I'm talking about, don't you?'

'Of ... of course. It's just the organisation has many clinical trials to manage, Mrs Colton.'

'That's no excuse for—'

'We'll call you as soon as we know more.'

'Dr Hartfield! At least tell him we love him and we're—'

'Yes, I'll tell him. Good day.'

Melissa dropped the telephone handset heavily onto its cradle and slumped against her desk. 'Oh, that woman. She's a mother hen. Tenth call of the day.'

Eddie smiled. 'They've been through a lot. Wouldn't *you* call incessantly if he were your kid? Besides, I thought you'd said you couldn't stand it when people over-exaggerated?'

Unable to stop the warmth creeping into her face, Melissa pursed her lips. 'Fine—*third* call'

'And what *are* you planning on telling the Principal Investigator when he returns from leave, given you've completely undermined his authority?'

Melissa narrowed her gaze. *Was that a veiled threat?* 'As institute director, it's *my* responsibility to investigate ethics concerns surrounding adverse event reports when the research group is being uncooperative, *especially* when those events raise serious concerns about the nature and safety of the therapy, *Eddie.*'

'I like it when you call me Eddie.'

'*Dr* Jonick, I told you, this has breached the agreement—not to mention Ramer's contact with a study participant—and is *doubly* of concern when it's a suspected biosafety matter and *I'm* the committee chair. Any fallout could destroy the institute's reputation.'

'And *this* doesn't breach it? What did the PI say when you presented these allegations?'

Tension worked into her jaw and her breathing grew quick and shallow. *Stop with the questions.* He'd already challenged her in front of the overenthusiastic junior researcher she'd enlisted to assist. 'He agreed it was a problem, but took no action—so *I* have.'

'But, Mel, this will implode the study.'

'The entire trial should have been terminated at first notification of Blaine's decline—' Eddie needn't know these events had only started *after* she'd incarcerated him. '—And Ramer's gone MIA. Can't get anything from his group, so if we don't figure this out before the PI's back, Blaine's out of luck—and so are we. I think we'd best get back to those results.'

Eddie flicked her a look laced with intent, but she merely adjusted her glasses and returned to the data in front of her. She worked hard to hide the twist of her intestines, which was anything but pleasant. Worse, Eddie always hinted that they should get to know each other better; engage more outside of work. On occasion he even commented on her perfume, so Melissa ensured she varied the fragrances she wore to keep him guessing.

When she was sure he was focussed on the report, she let her gaze slide over him. Broad shoulders and muscular chest effortlessly filling out a well-cut shirt. Pleasant hazel eyes, more green with yellow flecks, than brown. Full dark hair tussled into a modern style.

Sure, Eddie wasn't a bad specimen to look at and he justified his gym membership with frequent attendance, but there was just ... something. He was a brilliant researcher with considerably more experience than she had in genetic manipulations. Yet she often likened him to the tongue of a salivating dog—slightly abrasive and slimy.

She also needed him to finish what they'd started with Blaine. For that to occur, she had to ensure he never discovered her true reason for detaining Blaine. *Poor kid. Maybe I should have overdosed him when I had the chance.*

The conversation with Belinda Colton remained with Melissa long after she'd finished her meeting with Eddie. She'd checked through the records she'd managed to acquire, but couldn't find any drug in the copy of Blaine's treatment protocol, just some supplement— certainly none of the usual drugs used to control seizures. *Is the file incomplete?* Evidently these episodes had ceased after his successful gene therapy. Now they'd started again with increasing severity, Blaine could suffer irreversible damage if unmanaged. The question was, what had triggered them?

Belinda Colton said Ramer's group developed it.

She stopped typing details into the report she was working on and let this reality settle in her mind. Saving the half-completed document, she stood and headed for the door.

Melissa had just gowned up in the anteroom when she heard the alarms go off. She'd been right to have an observation room installed on her floor with Blaine in mind. No one seemed to have questioned the refurbishment, even so near a large suite of laboratories, and it enabled the direct access she required. Pulling on her respirator, she raced through the door and snapped on a pair of gloves. *Oh, the theatrics … But if I can get him to trust me, he might tell me what I need to know.*

'Blaine?' She jostled the boy's shoulder. He roused, but she could see he was approaching seizure once again. 'Blaine, don't go out on me. I need you to tell me what drug you're on. The ones we're using aren't working.'

Blaine's eyes rolled back in his head and Melissa prodded her finger against the panic button on the wall. *We can't lose him now. We're so close.*

'Blaine, tell me what it is. You can trust me.'

The room began to swarm with gowned people. The medic on call pushed in next to her and injected drugs through an i.v. cannula. She knew it would have little effect. *Come on, Blaine.* She glanced at the monitors as more pads and wires were rapidly connected. 'Are we getting this?'

'Yes. It's been the same each time, Mel—just longer.'

She watched Blaine's body writhe, clench and lose control. Until they knew *exactly* what they were dealing with, it could destroy him.

He passed the critical point and began to relax. But he was weaker than yesterday; paler than he had been after the previous episode. Each seizure was accelerating his decline.

'Carl.' She caught the eye of the attending medic. 'I need you to get the details of his treatment out of him. If we don't manage this *everything* will be in vain.' She held the eye of everyone present. 'You *know* what we're risking for this boy's sake. Don't make it for nothing.'

Don't make it for nothing. The information dream echoed through Blaine's head like a bell tolling through dense fog. The words were said with such urgency, such emotion, that a new respect for Melissa Hartfield spilled through him. Perhaps his wariness had been misguided. Perhaps her general detachment was a way of maintaining professionalism.

He felt blood leaving the vein in his arm and the spinning of his head increased. He was floating in an ocean, bobbing face down, deprived of oxygen and waiting for someone to turn him back over. His thoughts blurred as the dark hound of death paddled up to pull him further away from the shore. He screamed in his head, as he had when having this dream as a small child. In the instant before it would have been too late, he was turned over.

Melissa's blue eyes peered into his. She did not smile.

CHAPTER 7

'Damn!' Melissa thudded her fist against the desk. 'At this rate he'll die before we can get any clue of what Ramer transfected him with, let alone that mystery drug.'

'Why don't you ring the mother back and ask her to bring in the meds?'

Melissa eyed Eddie in disbelief. 'For a smart man you can be *really* brainless sometimes.' As much as he tried to hide it, she caught his flinch at her insult. Irrespective, she barrelled on. 'Remember that conversation where I told Belinda Colton I knew about the medication? Don't you think it'd cause her to ask some leading questions if suddenly I *didn't*?'

'Records could've been wrong.' Eddie shot back a smooth-as-syrup glance.

Yes, of course, he's right.

'Besides, you're the one who's good at bamboozling people with your intellectual brilliance, Mel. And if what you've said about Ramer is true—that he's breached the study agreement—'

'What do you mean by "*if*" it's true?'

Eddie shrugged. 'Ramer didn't strike me as the reckless, ignore procedure, type.'

'Clearly you didn't know him like I did.' Melissa's voice

remained confident, but she couldn't quite maintain eye contact.

'And why only Blaine? What about the other participants, if you're so worried about biosafety and such? Wouldn't it be more appropriate to raise it with the approving body and the committee?'

'Just remember who pays your bills, Eddie. If something this big blows up, so will ARI *and* your career. If we figure out how the therapy interacted for him, we'll know *exactly* what we're dealing with and can frame this to our advantage, and ARI's. *Then* we can worry about the others.'

'Let me guess how that scenario goes—Melissa Hartfield gets to play the rescuing superhero, while Merrick Ramer is revealed as the conniving villain? Sounds like a fairy-tale to me.'

She narrowed her eyes and glared. 'Very amusing. Just remember we're on a tight timeline, so how about fewer questions?'

Eddie clicked his tongue. 'Very well, m'lady, but I hope you're working on a good story for the PI when he's back from leave, because I'm pretty sure he's not going to see things in quite the same light.' He winked as he rose from his chair and exited the office with an infuriatingly casual stride.

Her cheeks burned. *Oh, Eddie, I'd drop you in a flash if I could.* He was a genius in the field of genomic medicine, but couldn't seem to land the research grants she found easy to obtain. This forced him to team up with her to keep his research going. But right now he was getting far too brazen for her liking. *And far too close to the truth.*

A debate ticked through her mind. *Should I call Belinda Colton? If I do, should I ask for the name and formulation of the medication, or request a sample?*

Requesting a sample would undoubtedly undermine every confidence in her abilities and prior statements, yet it would be the easiest way to enable analysis of the chemical formulation of the drug.

On the other hand, there was no way she wanted either of Blaine's parents near ARI—and his mother would insist on bringing it herself.

The Coltons had already challenged her professional judgment and justification for her handling of Blaine, simply because it countered the protocol outlined by Professor Ramer's group, as per the study agreement. They were asking far too many questions of her involvement with their son's trial. It proved they were not as naïve as she'd anticipated. No doubt they'd push even harder if she asked them to deliver drug samples, whilst refusing them access to Blaine. And were they to see their son? Melissa knew they would not be satisfied with Blaine's treatment, once they saw how swiftly he had declined. It would not be unlike them to raise their concerns with various authorities.

No, the Coltons must not become involved.

Despite this resolve, Melissa found herself passing an anxious half-hour before giving in and dialling the Colton's number. Blaine's mother picked up on the first ring.

'Mrs Colton, it's Melissa Hartfield. I'm sorry to bother you, but it seems Blaine's records haven't been updated properly or were incomplete. Unfortunately, with the Principal Investigator on leave, I have no way of validating the notes from his previous assessments.' She tapped her pen against the smooth surface of the desk as she paused to listen.

'That's strange, given ARI's extensive documentation processes. I would have expected this to be picked up months, even years, ago.'

'Agreed, it is strange, and I apologise it has taken this long to correct. As you know, I hadn't been with ARI long when Blaine's therapy was undertaken and wasn't involved with that work. I'm also not responsible for coordinating his trial, and the person who collated the initial documentation has since left.'

Melissa, don't overdo it—first the PI on holidays, now key staff leaving without conferring critical data?

'However, these inconsistencies have come to my attention as institute director, and it is my responsibility to correct this. It would be greatly beneficial if we could confirm the post-treatment recommendations and verify the product data described in the Investigator's Brochure.' She rushed on to evade the inevitable questions her fudged up explanation risked raising. 'Of course we've been managing Blaine's symptoms sufficiently, but we've had to use different drugs.'

'So, the protocol has been modified?'

'This is separate to that. Though it would be much easier if you could just tell me exactly what medication was prescribed to Blaine after the therapy.'

'Ramer's Cure.'

Melissa pulled the phone back, frowned at it, and then replaced it against her ear. 'I'm sorry, did you say *Ramer's Cure?*'

'Correct. The tablets are called Ramer's Cure. Do you need me to bring some to Blaine?'

She righted the pen and scribbled onto her note pad. 'That won't be necessary, Mrs Colton. But could you detail the composition?'

'No, I'm sorry. But it's the only medication he takes.'

'I see. Thanks for your help.'

Melissa pushed the 'end call' button so hard it hurt her finger. 'Ramer's Cure.'

She snorted and threw the phone down. Even the name of the drug mocked her. 'You might have been my superior for all those years, Ramer, but not anymore. I'll find out how you did it, just you wait.'

39

Blaine worked his hand down into the cargo pocket, just above his knee. The teeth of the open zipper rasped against his wrist. Yesterday's seizure had left him scarcely able to stand for a time, but he'd since taken the risk and gotten back into his own clothes. Because of his declining condition, the surveillance monitoring had increased. It appeared his suffering and consequential decline was of scientific significance.

He wasn't sure how much time had passed since the last round of white coats had left, but it had to be at least twenty minutes. Even alone, he was always conscious of the surveillance cameras in the room. He was certain even the balcony and bathroom now had movement sensors in them.

Pretending he was seeking an itch, with unsteady fingers he touched the small packet of tablets sitting against the bottom seam. He was relieved no one had found his secret weapon while it was stashed behind the loo.

He was determined to preserve them until he gained his freedom. If he couldn't get home he had no guarantee of obtaining another supply. He just hoped Dr Hartfield and her colleagues worked out a suitable alternative before he died or suffered permanent damage. If they didn't, he'd have to take a tablet simply to survive, let alone retain enough strength to get away.

Since the gene therapy, Blaine had never gone as long without Ramer's Cure. He wasn't quite sure what to expect. Having monitored his own condition, he'd noticed sleep enabled his body to recover somewhat, even delaying seizure at times. But if he wanted to stay alive, he knew it would only be a matter of time before he'd require the medication.

Unfortunately, Ramer's Cure didn't have an immediate action. It seemed the drug had to build up in his system over multiple doses before it took full effect. His parents had been given a five-year supply.

Five years.

Blaine wondered why they'd been issued such a large quantity at once. Then just six months after the gene therapy, he read in some news article that Professor Ramer, who'd developed the therapy, had resigned. Blaine hadn't heard anything about him since.

Did he know he'd get caught out?

He'd met Ramer once in a post-treatment follow-up. Due to his unexpected responsiveness, along with events beyond those indicated in the trial information pamphlet, his parents had pushed to get answers. But no one could explain *him*. They contacted regulating bodies, committees, nagged the Principal Investigator into a lather. After much rigmarole, by his fifteen-year-old standards, they were allowed a monitored consultation with the only expert who could answer some of their many questions: Professor Ramer.

A strained voice sounded at his door. 'Spot inspection. Quick, get him to the green or something.'

Melissa Hartfield.

Blaine zipped up the pocket and gingerly slid off the bed.

'Blaine.' The door burst open and Melissa, medic Carl and one of the security guards who had chased him that first day rushed into the room. *No face masks, no gloves, no personal protection at all.* Was it all a façade?

'Can you walk yet, Blaine?'

Dr Hartfield kept her distance, but he recognised desperation when he saw it. *Opportunity time.* 'I could if you let me ring my parents, then ...'

He didn't finish. Melissa threw his jacket at him and the men hauled him out of the observation unit. He writhed and kicked but had little strength. All he achieved was complete exhaustion.

'Where are you taking me? Let go!'

'Shut up, kid.'

'Or what, Baldy?'

'Blaine, please cooperate. You know that regulating body I mentioned? We've just found out they've authorised a spot inspection, with inspectors only minutes away. Remember, if they find out about you ...'

The statement hung unfinished, but Blaine silently substituted 'destroy the unauthorised GMO'. He still couldn't figure out why Carl and Baldy didn't seem worried by his potentially infectious state. Instead of wasting effort on it, he took the opportunity to scan their exit path—*my exit path, next time.*

There was the lab. He spotted an instrument room on the same side as the observation facility in which he was being held. Glancing back, he noticed he hadn't heard the door of the anteroom latch.

How careless, Dr Hartfield.

Clearly, they could crack under pressure. In seconds, the door alarm bleated an alert. Blaine watched Dr Hartfield rush back to push it shut that last fraction.

Other labs came off the corridor. *Tissue culture 1* was plastered beside the door of one room. The next lab sported a large PC-2 and biohazard sign and was marked *Virology*. A little further on they reached a T-intersection. The passage to the right was blocked by secured double doors, placarded with various restrictions and biohazard warnings.

They turned left.

Blaine knew he hadn't been brought in this way. *Surely they aren't going to take me right out the front door? Why risk it if I'm a biohazard?*

Seconds later he was carted into an elevator. Dr Hartfield swiped her card across a reader and plugged in 'R'. He barely had time to wonder what it meant before he was dragged out onto the roof and directed past a modern garden, towards a small expanse of lawn. The grass was close-cropped, and a fancy water feature bubbled into a lap pool a short distance away. Near it was a barbeque and bar, both under a pergola that would look more at home on a Pacific Island, than in Brisbane's latest version of Technology Park.

When Baldy and Carl let him go, he realised Dr Hartfield wasn't with them. A cool breeze whisked across the rooftop and Blaine was pleased she had thrown his hooded jacket at him. *No incriminating evidence.* He shrugged it on.

Glancing up, he noticed clouds gathering like a dark scowl. It reflected his general disposition. *More than that, it'll inconvenience Baldy and Carl. That pergola isn't going to protect them from a serious downpour.* With a brief scan, Blaine tried to gain his bearings. *I wonder if there's a fire escape somewhere?*

CHAPTER 8

'Excuse me, while I mute that.' Melissa had tried ignoring her office phone, but this was the fourth time it had rung in as many minutes.

The inspectors, evidently satisfied with the facility and its practices, were rounding up the final remarks of their report. She reached across her desk to mute the ringtone, anxious to end the inspection *without* further interruption.

'Dr Hartfield, we can wait if you need to take that.'

'No, this matter is more important.'

One of the inspectors deflected her concern with a small wave of their hand. 'Go ahead. It's not a problem. Clearly your attention is required by someone.'

With a tight smile, she lifted the receiver with a grip firmer than necessary.

'Dr Hartfield, it's Corelli from switch. I know your schedule says you're unavailable, but I've got Belinda Colton on the line—again. She's been calling *constantly* all morning. Could you *please* speak to her?'

'I'm sorry, but I'm—'

'She won't stop ringing. As soon as I tell her you're unavailable, she just dials again. I have to put her through. She's congesting the line.'

'Now is not a—'

'Dr Hartfield? It's Belinda Colton. I want to know where our son is. He had his 33-month follow-up over three weeks ago, with apparently no significant points of note. Yet, after this unscheduled appointment, you've now held Blaine for over a week for no good reason, without *any* communication from the Principal Investigator or notification of change to his trial protocol. *Tell me* what is going on.'

The demand was so loud both inspectors looked up. Melissa came to her feet; certain they would know exactly who was on the phone. She turned away. Even then, she felt the two pairs of eyes scanning her back. 'Mrs Colton, I can hear you're upset. Perhaps it would be best if I called you back later.'

'No. I've already rung the hospital *and* clinical trials unit, and Blaine's not listed as an inpatient. I do *not* believe you are being honest with me, and I'll keep calling until you tell me where you've got him. If you don't, I'll be on your doorstep in as little time as it takes to drive there, and I won't be quiet about it.'

Melissa took a slow, deep breath—which took more effort than usual, given she felt like the woman's fingers had reached through the telephone and were wrapped around her throat. Looking over her shoulder, she tried to provide a silent reassurance for the inspectors.

Clearing her throat, she again turned her back on them. 'Mrs Colton, I explained the tests wouldn't take very long.'

'When I called yesterday, you said he might be there a week longer. Which is it?'

She pressed the handset harder to her ear, hoping the woman's sharp words couldn't be overheard. Perspiration dotted her lip, and she carefully brushed it away, relieved her shirt was a breathable fabric. *Think, Melissa, think!*

Under no circumstances did she want the investigators sighting or speaking with Blaine. All she wanted to do was end the call, only she knew that if she did the phone was start ringing again in under a minute. *Could leave it off the hook?* But first, she had to get Belinda Colton off the line.

'Um, Blaine left the facility mid-morning.' It was *nearly* true. He'd been taken to the rooftop green. 'As I said previously, some tests were inconclusive, so the investigator wanted to be certain of where he was in his progress.'

'And?'

Melissa stopped, carefully arranging soothing words in her head before she let them loose. 'Well, as always, it's important for you and Mr Colton to receive a comprehensive report, along with a face-to-face consultation. I'm confident the Principal Investigator will arrange this once your husband is back from his trip.'

'That doesn't explain where my son is.' Belinda's tone was low and brittle.

Melissa felt building pressure in her lungs. She needed to complete her business with the inspectors. She'd never known them to be unreasonable in her previous dealings, but she'd never been subject to a spot inspection before—*and had never flaunted the rules so blatantly in the past*. Had Belinda Colton been in touch with them?

Unlikely, but anything was possible. If they had to wait much longer, they just might become more interested in her conversation than necessary.

'I understand Blaine seemed keen on getting home.' *Also true.* 'But you know what teenagers can be like. Perhaps he met up with someone. Would he have gone via a friend's house?'

'He's not come home, Dr Hartfield. I said that. Are you certain he's not still there somewhere?'

Melissa glanced again at the waiting inspectors. 'I'm ... I'm quite certain. In fact, if you checked our closed-circuit footage, I'm sure there'd be video surveillance of him leaving the building.'

Melissa, what is wrong *with you? Why'd you say that?*

Everything else she'd said was a slight extension of the truth. With an outright lie, she knew she was panicking. Foolish statements like that begged for litigation.

'Could he have run off somewhere?' *I've made it worse.* As soon as she spoke, she felt an eerie coldness hit her from the other end of the line. It was like chilled air spilling from an open freezer.

'Blaine's not like that, Dr Hartfield. He's a good boy. Could ...' There was a moment's hesitation. 'Could you have told him some bad news?'

'I'm so sorry, Mrs Colton, I'd really like to help, but I'm a little tied up right now. Perhaps I can return your call shortly? I'm sure he'll be home soon.'

'Fine. I'll await your call.'

'Thank you.'

Melissa's fear pupated from a grub-sized worry to a fully-grown, flailing moth of anxiety as the investigators asked more questions. She was stupid to have answered the phone in the first place. Like the rest of the country, they'd heard about Blaine's progress and were astonished by his remarkable response, against other participants. Despite every effort at confidentiality, nothing had been able to keep this phenomenal result from the media.

Melissa latched onto this point. 'That's exactly what the investigator's trying to determine. I'm sure you can appreciate how this process has been hindered by Professor Ramer's sudden resignation. I understand he's still a co-contact for the collaborative research group, but his availability has been inconsistent since he left ARI.'

She watched them closely, measuring their reactions to ensure that, as far as they were concerned, her explanation fell reasonably within the spectrum of due process. A crease started forming on the brow of one inspector—the type that would deepen into a crevice-like frown that only acceptable answers to countless more questions would smooth. *Time to change the topic.*

'If you're familiar with Mitochondrial Disease, you'd appreciate the variability of each case, depending on the degree and type of genetic mutation; whether it's a mutation in the nuclear or mitochondrial DNA; the loci on which the defective gene—or genes—sit. There are many different types of mitochondria-related disorders. Some individuals can be minimally affected by their condition, while for others it presents as a life-threatening illness.'

Melissa stopped. She sounded like an insecure, fresh-faced graduate delivering a lecture to promote her intellectual superiority. It was more than likely these people knew these facts, but she'd gone on and on. Immediately she changed tack. 'It's my understanding that, despite Blaine Colton's debilitating condition, he doesn't specifically fit the recognised disease categories. Not exactly. But he's lucky. By some miracle the damage to his system over time seems minimal, and it is believed the gene therapy happened to be a perfect, or close enough, patch for the mutated regions.'

'That single intervention achieved a sustainable result, even with such a complex combination of mutations? Incredible.'

Then the second inspector voiced their observations. 'You seem quite familiar with the protocol.'

She coughed. Nearly choked. Then offered a thin laugh. 'Ah … not really—it's just what I've observed … summary reports, ethics committee approvals, some essential documents passing my desk as the institution head … you know?'

The investigators glanced at each other, before the nosey-parker one kept burrowing for information. 'You were telling his mother the assessment schedule has been altered? Is there a safety issue?'

Melissa took a long breath and let silence hang. This wasn't how she'd expected it to go. No other subjects had experienced long-term success and she debated whether or not it would go better for her if she said Blaine was following this same projection. She decided the inspectors would only ask more questions if he was supposedly fine after nearly a week of follow-up tests.

'Well, um ... the Principal Investigator is on leave and ... essentially, yes—well, possibly. It seems either the treatment may be breaking down, or it has a limited efficacy, just as for the other participants who experienced short-term improvement.' *I probably shouldn't know that ...* Her body had grown so warm even her legs were sweating. The hole she'd dug with her half-truths barely left her head above ground.

'There have been communications with the collaborative group?'

'Certainly.' *When hell freezes over.* There was no way Melissa intended communicating *any* of her actions with Ramer's group.

More questions followed and she managed to negotiate each one, working hard to dodge further statements that might suggest everything was not quite as it seemed, nor that Blaine's extended testing was involuntary. With some vague references to ethics concerns and adverse events, they finally quit the interrogation. But she knew she'd made another blunder and severely underestimated the knowledge of the biosafety inspectors on clinical trial protocol. *What if they dig further?*

By the time they left, she felt like a disintegrating length of used paper towel. She bored her pen into the top page of her notepad.

Everything was going fine until that woman rang.

She pressed her palms against her forehead. Each word of the conversation re-played through her mind. She knew she'd crossed a line she could never uncross. Worse, she had to return the call and repair as many of the holes in her lies as possible.

CHAPTER 9

Blaine lay on the lawn and pretended to doze in the winter sun. The gathering clouds had come to nothing and promptly dispersed. The grass, which he'd expected to be crisp and cool like the air, was fake. He could barely support his own weight, could hardly raise his arms, and was tempted to take a half dose of Ramer's Cure to manage his condition.

He took the opportunity to examine his surroundings: listening, inhaling, watching through half-hooded eyelids. He looked for any possible escape path. Based on the occurrence of the seizures, he knew he'd been captive more than a week. The frequency of the seizures would inevitably increase without the Cure.

He *had* to get out—before he was too weak to attempt it.

From all appearances, the faux green space was fully enclosed by a concrete wall with a metre more of glass on top. Undoubtedly a safety measure. A modern building constructed to modern health and safety regulations. There definitely had to be a fire escape somewhere.

Yawning, he rolled onto his flank, as if sunning the opposite side of his body. Again, through slotted eyes, he traced the perimeter with his gaze.

Yes! There. Fire exit stairs—clearly signed.

Six ticks for hope.

Carl was standing between him and it, as if nonchalantly surveying the scene.

Yawning, Blaine stretched out and did fall asleep for a while. He was woken by Baldy's firm shake to his shoulder.

'Wake up, kid. Time to go.'

Blaine squinted at the large man's hand and rubbed his eyes. 'How'd you get those marks on your wrist?'

'Huh?' A UHF communication radio on Baldy's belt burbled in subdued tones.

'Sam, hurry up.'

Baldy was called Sam—and Sam ignored Blaine's question about the scars as he hauled him to his feet. Blaine studied Sam's hand and was certain the marks were from having numerous i.v. lines inflicted upon him.

Perhaps Sam knew what it was like to be a human pincushion. Perhaps Sam was only tough on the outside. Or maybe he was a druggie.

'Have to take the stairs, Carl. Network's just gone down.' Sam directed them through a door. *The* door.

Blaine was relieved his power nap had injected a little more strength into his limbs, or he'd be tumbling down like a crash-test dummy. He glanced at the emergency evacuation procedures plastered on each level as they descended the fire exit stairwell.

'Stupid swipe cards. Good thing you carry master keys. Keys never go down.' Carl's voice echoed up and down the fireproof cement walls.

'Anyone allocated a key'll have it out now for sure. Downtime messes with the instruments and phonelines, too. That means Dr Hartfield will be exceptionally happy when we return her little lab rat.'

Blaine frowned at Sam, but the huge man winked back. *Lab rat? Did they sympathise? Was it worth the risk?* 'You guys gonna let me go all the way down? I'd really like to go home.' He grinned to help convince them.

'Now, young Blaine, that seems a reasonable request, but I don't think my mortgage repayments would look so good without a job.'

'You're just going to put me back against my will and let those vampires get at me again?'

'That's the way it'll be.'

'Could you ...' Blaine felt like he'd swallowed an invisible ball from the air. He tried to push it down far enough to finish his sentence. He could see there were just a few floors to go, so he coughed, gulped, and tried again. 'Could you please call my mum to tell her I miss her and Dad, and that I'm okay?' He gritted his jaw to force the ball firmly down.

Was he okay?

He knew in and instant the lump could bounce back up and set off a whole chain of carefully squelched responses.

'I'm sure Dr Hartfield will see to that.'

But from the look Carl and Sam shot each other, Blaine was pretty certain they were unconvinced of any such thing. He shrugged as they opened the door and steered him indoors. 'Thanks anyway.'

He took mental notes about the alternate route back to his room. He recognised Melissa Hartfield's office and glimpsed the lab through a glass wall behind her desk. Intrigued, he pretended to lose his footing so he could look a little longer. She was facing away, a mobile phone to her ear, looking through the glass at the laboratory staff whose work had stagnated.

It seemed the network outage hadn't just messed with the swipe card access and landlines. From the untidy sprawl of computer-linked equipment, Blaine guessed it messed with just about everything that could be networked.

Then his preternaturally-acute hearing picked up Dr Hartfield's voice—and he froze.

'Well, Mrs Colton, as I explained, some of the tests were inconclusive. They suggested his treatment could be starting to fail, that in a matter of months he could be back in a chair, or even ... well, I'd not like to presume. Observations confirm his health is declining rapidly.'

In the stillness from the network outage, he could even pick up the soft sob on the other end of the phone.

'I'm sorry. I would have told you sooner, but we only just received the results back this morning. I was in the middle of an important meeting when you called earlier, so was unable to discuss this confidential information. If you have any questions, I'd be happy to meet with you both to determine how we can make Blaine most comfortable in the coming period. Good day.'

Dr Hartfield placed the mobile phone on her desk and leaned back in her chair. As she looked up, she seemed startled to see Blaine's eyes probing her.

'Come on, kid.' Sam jostled him along as Dr Hartfield stood up. Blaine heard the slam of her office door moments later.

Mum!

How desperately he wanted to speak to her. What must she think after *that* prognosis? He knew it wasn't true and the only reason they'd be getting such indications would be due to the omission of Ramer's Cure from his treatment.

Or could Dr Hartfield be lying outright?

This thought planted itself in his mind. *If so, why?*

Didn't she claim my parents were the ones who had lied?

Sam and Carl directed him through a corridor thick with the aroma of disinfectant. That ball in Blaine's throat began to roll around, tearing like a lump of gravel. It was all he could do not to run back to Dr Hartfield's office and tell her about 'The Cure' on the off-chance it meant he could go home and get the medication he so desperately needed. But instinct told him it would only extend the sampling and pose more questions for them to answer.

Without warning, Sam gripped Blaine's arm, pulling him to a stop. 'Carl, double check they're ready for him.' He unlocked the door and pushed it open for his colleague.

With a nod, Carl passed through, leaving them standing against the wall. As the door slowly closed, Blaine heard a monitor squealing. He recognised the pitch and, based on the direction, decided it was probably one of the machines in his room.

Networked.

The sound muted as the door shut. Blaine took the opportunity to study Sam's profile. Tattoos scrawled across Sam's arms. Most of them were poorly executed. They looked faded. A few scars and the odd angle of Sam's nose suggested he'd had a fair bit of opportunity to talk with his fists in the past. But like the faded tattoos, the scars seemed old—white rather than angry red.

'Why aren't you scared of me, Sam?'

Sam glanced sidewards, a half-frown wrinkling his brow. 'The coats don't do much for me, plus we didn't want the authorities getting funny about things if they saw us.'

Blaine grinned.

'What's with you, kid?'

'I call 'em "coats" too.'

Sam returned his grin. 'Coats attract attention. Without them, we could just be taking some school kid on a tour. 'Sides, I figure

55

your folks haven't had much of an issue with you, so I'm safe. Just don't bite.' He winked.

Sam's all right. And I think I've just made a friend inside.

Seven ticks.

The door sprung ajar and Carl's head popped through the gap. He grinned, held up a key and waggled it at them. 'Just resetting the cameras an' gear. Won't be a minute. Phones are back up now, too.'

'What a dumb system.' Blaine snorted his disapproval.

'You don't say. Recent addition that cost ten human kidneys to have put in.'

Blaine loved the shot of sarcasm as much as the hint of a conscience behind it. 'I'm thinking it's the same system my dad has at his work. He's always having trouble because of it.'

'Probably, kid, probably.'

Finally they were allowed in. Blaine began to count the seconds until the door clicked behind them. He needed to know just how much time he'd have before the alarm went off.

But it didn't click. He strained his ears, wondering if he'd missed it.

Must have. The alarm hasn't sounded.

Then he heard a voice at the far end of the corridor. 'Where's Cable? We need these door alarms reset.'

'Our guy's on holidays. Have to get someone sent over from another division—and there's a scheduled maintenance Thursday. At this rate we'll get nothing done this week.'

Thursday. Eight ticks!

Blaine's heart jumped in his chest as he calculated what day it was. *Tuesday? Or Wednesday? But, if Wednesday, surely they'd have said 'tomorrow'.* He figured he had at most 48 hours to make his move.

As soon as Carl and Sam left, he went to the bathroom and took one dose of Ramer's Cure, feeling as if all his hopes had collided at once. Tomorrow he'd take another Cure and then wait for opportunity to strike.

CHAPTER 10

It was Thursday morning. Blaine tried not to bound from his bed and jump out to the balcony. He felt much better. The Cure was starting to take effect.

Even though he had no deodorant, there would be no showering this morning. He'd happily put up with his stale slept-in smell rather than miss his chance at freedom. His clothes also hadn't been laundered since the spot inspection. Despite several offers to have them washed, there was no way was he going to get caught escaping in a hospital gown.

Whistling, he put on his shoes and waited for the usual entourage to appear.

'Morning, young Blaine.'

'Hi Carl.' Carl was back in full protective garb. Blaine wondered if he'd been required to burn the clothes he'd worn when escorting him upstairs with Sam.

The medic made the usual observations. At the end, he stood back and studied Blaine with gloved hands-on hips. 'Feeling better now, are we? Temp's relatively stable and no seizures for two days.'

Unable to help himself, Blaine flashed a grin. 'Yeah, it's a good week.' If he'd still had his wallet and phone, it would have been perfect. *Perfect for escape, that is.*

Shaking his head, Carl recorded the readings from each monitor and promptly disconnected the units. 'No point having them going off when the system goes down—which should be soon.'

'Do they stop working?'

'No. When the computers aren't networked, it throws a server error and the alarms start to squeal. It's the way it's set up, for now. But I'm thinking you're not going to need them for today anyway. Good to see, kid.'

'Could you show me?'

Carl ran through each sensor and described what it did. Blaine had spent enough time in care to already know it all, but he needed Carl to provide him with a card. 'Hey, can I have that?'

'What, your report?'

'It's just a copy, isn't it? I feel like doing some writing.'

Understanding registered in Carl's eyes. 'Sorry, Blaine. I'd not even considered how bored you might be here. I thought you were too sick to care.'

'Even some cards would be good. Unlike most of my generation, I can actually play Solitaire without a computer.' Blaine gave another cheesy grin. 'You can incinerate them when I'm done.'

Carl chuckled. 'I'll see what I can do. Just give me a minute.'

Blaine swung between panic the network would go down before Carl returned and fear there were no cards in the facility. *I wouldn't put it past anyone banning poker here.*

It was several minutes before Carl returned. 'Found this in the tea room.' He plonked a game of Monopoly onto a lowset table set against the wall. 'Sorry, it was the best I could do. Maybe you could play against yourself?'

'Thanks, Carl.' *Perfect.* Monopoly cards would work just as well.

Of habit, just as his mother had taught him to do as a child, he counted another tick for hope, adding it to his growing tally. *Nine.*

Melissa gathered her special operations team together. At least, that was how she referred to them. A more accurate description of the three handpicked researchers sitting opposite her at the conference table in her office was: gullible—the young female PhD candidate always trying to impress her; manipulable—the mid-career underachiever who took her at her word and never asked questions; and coerced—Eddie, which was a gentler approach than all out blackmail. So long as they *thought* they knew what was happening, she could continue to garner their collaboration. Except for Eddie. He was making her nervous.

Besides Sam in security, and Carl, all other staff were on a need-to-know basis. Even Carl and Sam had only enough details to secure their cooperation. The other staff generally accepted Blaine was undergoing some post-treatment follow-up tests due to some safety concerns about his therapy. Nothing more.

Time was critical. She was no closer to discovering the intimate details of Ramer's gene therapy success, and Blaine could not be held forever. She just hoped he never questioned her claim they had the right to keep him there. It was a substantial extension of the truth and had nothing to do with regulating bodies or any other government organisation.

Dr Jonick held the floor. 'I'm convinced the key is in those Cure meds Belinda Colton mentioned. Whatever it is, it keeps the whole thing balanced.'

'Well, Eddie, I think you've just booked yourself an assignment.' Melissa raised an eyebrow as Eddie's face swung towards her. 'Don't we still have the same pharmacist as when Ramer's group was on site? Aren't you chummy with him?' She smiled. 'Since you won't be able to do any other work soon enough, why don't you go and have a chat? See what you can discover about any custom combinations run through the tablet press, say, three years ago for a certain Professor Ramer's research group.'

Eddie's glare was half-mocking, half-provocative. 'There's something else I've noticed. Here. Check these counts.' He slid a copy of some graphed results across the table. 'I don't like what I'm seeing. Has the Principal Investigator flagged this previously?'

Melissa ignored him, for she had no idea what he was talking about and didn't want to lose face. Instead, she turned away to address the two other scientists. 'We must remember our goal— determine the intricacies of the therapy so we can understand why it is causing these adverse events. With the agreement breached due to the collaborative group's lack of cooperation and Ramer's "non communiqué" in response to serious participant safety concerns, it's not only an ethics noncompliance, but a matter of life and death for Blaine.'

She congratulated herself on the level of conviction she projected. She could nearly convince herself of these claims. 'I've instructed Sam to befriend him, but evidently Blaine hasn't mentioned anything about the meds. Carl's also had little success.' She would see the medic and security guard when this meeting was done.

'Dr Hartfield, I've got the last set of results, but there's nothing remarkable.'

Melissa reached across the table to accept the report from the other woman. In the corner of her eye she saw Eddie push back his chair. By the time she turned her head, he was stalking to the door. The line of his back told her she'd offended him. She thought for a moment of calling him back. But before she'd decided whether it was in her best interests to pacify him, he was gone.

Eddie looked through some old tablet press usage logs.

'That all you need, Ed?'

'Yeah, thanks, Len.'

'Just don't go playing with the press. You have no idea how temperamental that lovely lady can be.' He cast an eye over the mechanical contraption that punched tablets from powdered drug stocks.

'I know, Len. I know.'

'And if you need to ask anything, I'll be in my office across the way.'

'Great.'

Eddie flicked through the logbook until he found a series of orders for Professor Ramer's research group. The dates indicated a six-month period leading up to Blaine's gene therapy. Each one had a series of codes, but they didn't seem like chemical formulas. If they were shorthand for a drug, it wasn't one he'd heard of before.

'Hey, Len?' Eddie blew a kiss to Len's 'lovely lady' and headed across the corridor. 'Did you make these up?'

Len came to the door. 'Oh, that's Professor Ramer's "Cure". No, he wouldn't let me near it.'

'What does this stand for?' Eddie pointed at the description column. 'RC-M-X2.'

'That was Ramer's code. I think it stood for Ramer's Cure modification X2. Don't ask me what the "X2" was for, 'cause I don't know.'

Eddie stopped. 'X2?' He started to laugh. 'X2. The supplement. We thought it indicated two vitamin supplements per day, not a drug code. But why would he call it a supplement?'

'Mate, you're talking to yourself.' Len clapped Eddie's shoulder and chuckled.

Eddie shook his head and offered a half-smile. 'So who made them up?'

'Ramer did.'

'Himself? The whole mix?'

'Yeah. Wanted to handle the scaled-up prep for the clinical trials within his team. Said it was too important to risk anyone else taking the blame, if it wasn't right. Did up quite a few batches in the end. Enough to medicate half of Queensland.' Len threw back his head and laughed loudly.

Eddie continued to stare at the dates and usage records. 'Do you have any samples? Even just a powdered stock?'

Len shook his head. 'He set it up, mixed his own batches, punched them out, and cleaned it up—except for once.'

'And who was that?' Eddie waited, thinking he might finally have some news that could put him in Melissa's good books. Now there was a lovely lady he'd like to impress—despite the fact she'd just blown him off. *Let her figure out the results herself.*

'That young research assistant Ramer had for a while.'

'You mean, Luke Kastenholz, the RA he had before he left?'

'Yeah, that's the one. Both resigned about the same time, remember?'

For the first time Eddie really thought about this fact. Both Ramer and Kastenholz had left within days of each other.

What did that mean, if anything?

He shook his head, realising he was indulging a wild, invalidated notion. 'So what did Professor Ramer get Luke to do?'

'Just assist. But he'd have known what they were handling. Was a smart one, that Luke.' A deep crease rutted Len's brow. 'But why are you asking me? Ramer's group's notes are probably locked up somewhere gathering dust. And the product they prepared would've been registered with the relevant association and documented for the trials. So why don't you just ask the PI?'

'He's on leave, but yeah, you're right.'

Eddie felt like he'd tried to bench press too much weight and the bar was hard on his chest. He'd made Len suspicious, but there was no help for it. He cringed to think what the pharmacist might say if he knew how low he'd sunk to stay hitched to the Hartfield research wagon. *I'm in way over my head.*

What was he doing snooping for restricted information on an investigational product from a clinical trial agreement with a collaborative research group in which he had no part? It didn't matter that the group had operated out of a laboratory within the same organisation, it was a legally separate entity. Melissa's claims as the institute director held some validity, *if* what she said about Ramer was true, but something wasn't right. Something *beyond* the involuntary restraint of a minor. It was a constant feeling of hauling an extra ten kilos on each shoulder.

'Ed, it's been a while since you've dropped by. Everything okay?' Len folded his arms and reclined with a casual lean against the door jamb.

Eddie looked away. Len had been a great friend when he'd first joined ARI. The pharmacist could read him like a book. In fact, he was the only colleague who knew the *real* reason behind Eddie's abrupt return to Brisbane after years of working in Melbourne. Perhaps that was why Len judged his behaviour less harshly than most.

'Busy. You know.' He shrugged.

'Vague, evasive. You know.'

Eddie faced him. 'Look, Len, things have been different since Ramer left.'

'No kidding.' He let out a low whistle. 'I remember the day that determined little blonde marched in here with her entourage of researchers. Made no secret of her ambitions to outdo her former supervisor.'

'Wonder if Professor Ramer knew how seriously she'd take that challenge?' Eddie's gaze drifted to a distant point. 'One year. That's all the time it took for him to tender his resignation after her arrival.'

'And for her to be appointed Director in Ramer's place.' Len shook his head. 'I liked Ramer. He never thought so much of himself that he couldn't take time for the little people. Always seemed genuinely interested, even though his life was one constant schedule of meetings and deadlines.'

Eddie nodded. 'Yeah, he was approachable. But Mel is, too. She's just got different priorities.'

'Look.' Len shifted his position. 'I know you think she's a bit all right, but Ed, there's something ... not right about her.'

Oh, Len, if only you knew ... Eddie almost shrank back as he considered his own swift entanglement with the appealing Dr Hartfield.

His research funds acquired while ARI was under Ramer's directorship had been ending, marking the cessation of his projects. And then Melissa had reached out, suggesting they collaborate. Given she had a knack of finding the pot of gold when it came to research grants, he figured there was nothing to lose. One of her guarantees had been an assurance he'd still have some say in the direction of the projects they collaborated on. In reality, she signed off on any grant applications and he had to toe the line according to *her* priorities. He was increasingly required to advance Melissa's research interests, while his got pushed further down the list.

Since getting caught in her most recent scheme, Eddie could scarcely look Len in the eye. So he'd started avoiding him.

'Ed?' Len's voice drew Eddie back to the present. 'If you ever want to grab a drink or just hang out with m'lady o' the tablet press—'

'But don't touch her?' He handed the records back to Len, who grinned.

'You know where I am. And I promise not to breathe a word of the latest gossiping gabbers' instalment.'

Eddie scoffed. *Yeah, I know what people say about me and my 'dates'. Let them talk.* But as much as he pretended otherwise, it did barb him—and Len knew that. 'Thanks. I'll try and get up here more often.'

He returned to the lift, deep in thought. At the last moment he stopped short of pressing the button and checked his watch. *Has the network gone down yet? Do I even care?* No, today he'd take the stairs. In fact, he felt like a nice long walk away from ARI—and its beautiful Chief Scientist.

His echoing footsteps boomed up and down the stairwell, from the basement to the roof top green. Len's final question sat like a shadow in the corner of his mind.

Had the records from Ramer's research group remained at ARI when he resigned? Had they been deposited with the funding body? Some IP agreements dictated research notes must remain in a secured location at the institute that owned the IP, under a designated authority. *Was that authority Melissa?* Highly unlikely, knowing Ramer. He wouldn't have been so careless as to let his notes fall into the hands of his overambitious former PhD student and now number one rival, Melissa Hartfield. And given the trial was ongoing, he expected the group was still active. *Was Ramer still heading it?*

And what of the RA? Why hadn't anyone noticed he had resigned just days before Ramer's abrupt resignation and disappearance? Had something gone down within the group? Could Luke be the link they were seeking?

He knew Melissa wasn't going to be pleased with his findings. In fact, he was certain she'd be livid.

CHAPTER 11

When Dr Hartfield stalked in with Sam in tow, then directed Carl to follow them out, Blaine knew it was the best chance he would have. The probability of it coinciding with the network downtime seemed too perfect to believe. Only problem was, now that the machines had been disconnected, how would he know when it occurred?

Step 1: Reconnect the monitors Carl had detached. He fiddled and pushed buttons on the one he knew squealed—then waited. That way he'd know the instant the outage happened.

One thing Blaine was certain of—he didn't want to cross Dr Hartfield. She'd clomped in with scarlet cheeks and eyes as fiery as a welder's torch, then practically marched the two men out. He heard Sam mutter something to Carl about some meeting not going well. *Whatever.* There was something seriously up with her today.

A pulsing shriek interrupted Blaine's thoughts. *Make that ten ticks ...*

A man in surgical scrubs barged in. 'I thought Carl turned that off?'

Blaine tried not to grin.

'Did you touch that, kid? Why is it reconnected?'

'I was just trying to see how it worked.'

'Well, leave it alone, will you?'

'All right.'

Step 2: Let the man do his thing then follow him to the door but keep far enough back not to attract attention.

The attendant fumbled a key into the rarely used lock, then pulled on the heavy panel and exited. *Swipe card fail. Eleven ticks. If I could just get a hold of that key ...* Blaine waited for the door to automatically close.

Step 3: At the last possible moment, shove a card between the face and strike plates where the latch usually catches.

He reached forward and only just made it. He hoped a Monopoly card would be enough to prevent the door from shutting properly.

The biggest challenge in Blaine's mind was the exiting man. *Would he notice the interfering card?*

With the network down the door shouldn't alarm, but still he held his breath and waited.

No siren yet.

The man glanced back and jumped when he saw Blaine wave at him through the viewing glass. Removing his protective gear, he washed up and left the anteroom.

Blaine watched closely. Just as he'd hoped, there was no need for a swipe card to exit through the external door.

Still no siren.

Blaine's shoulders sagged as his lungs emptied in a rush. *Twelve ticks.* He was fairly certain that man was on duty observing him this shift. He smiled when he saw him head off down the corridor. Probably to the tearoom. *Thirteen.*

Step 4: open the door.

Blaine pulled on it. The card dropped out as it opened, and he flicked it back towards the bed with the toe of his shoe. *Fourteen and gone.*

Crouched down, he waddled out of sight below the half-glass wall.

As soon as he was in the clear, he sprinted out the same way Sam and Carl had brought him in on Tuesday. He could hear Dr Hartfield's raised voice in her office, but he had no time to eavesdrop.

He dashed to the stairwell and practically skidded down the stairs until he reached a large number 3. In that moment the world paused. This was it. This was the link to where his life had changed forever.

Despite the foolishness of it, he cracked open the door and peered out. Unlike the level he'd escaped, there was no security on this door. *Public access because of its link to the hospital and clinical trials unit maybe?* Triple-checking the coast was clear, he stepped through the portal and walked dreamlike through the enclosed walkway connecting ARI to the clinical trials unit. Stepping up to a glass wall, his hand shook as he placed his splayed fingers against the pane.

Inside the room were three severely debilitated boys. He watched them closely as they awaited their turn to go beyond, into the treatment room.

That was me three years ago.

Trapped in his own body with his own thoughts. Unable to believe his parents' assurance of love and worth. *What good was I then?*

What good are they?

Blaine fell back a step, unable to believe the thought that had shot through his head. How could he, now able to live what they were only dreaming of, as swiftly forget what it was to be stuck in that weak, ailing body? Hope had been a glowing ember in the bottom of a canyon. So faint, he often failed to see its light.

But what if I could help find the answer for them?

A tug-of-war began within him. Was he being selfish running away? Could his life, even if restricted to a facility, reveal the secret those kids needed to unlock their own freedom?

A carer glanced up and saw him looking. He backed away from her stare and from the three pairs of eyes that rolled involuntarily for lack of strength, the dribble that clustered at the corners of muscle-weakened mouths, the limbs that did little more than flap at peculiar moments, as if controlled by an unseen puppeteer—or like him, had largely no movement at all. Slowly he retreated until he found himself backed against the stairwell door. Turning, he rammed it open and fled.

He careened, unthinking, all the way to the ground-floor car park. Just metres barred the way between him and freedom—along with two security guards on the car park boom gate.

Crouched beside a low concrete wall, Blaine scanned the area for options. He knew security could already have been notified of his absence. Yet, by the way the guards joked and talked, it was unlikely.

He was still deciding what to do when the top of a glossy red VW convertible folded down right before his eyes. He waited as it started to back out, hardly able to believe his luck. The driver had to wait as another car pulled into a park a few spaces down, on the opposite side. Clearly she recognised the other driver and, waving to catch their attention, hopped out.

Bonus ticks.

The instant her back was turned, Blaine jumped into the back seat and curled himself into a tight ball on the floor. He dragged a backpack across to partially cover himself, and hoped neither the driver nor guards would notice him.

It was only a minute before the woman returned. Thankfully she didn't look closely at the rear seat of her car.

They moved towards the exit, the engine purring like a contented cat.

'Have a great day, ma'am.'

'You too.'

They continued forward and Blaine glanced up as they passed under the boom gate.

Step 5: Freedom!

The car accelerated with a torque he'd never experienced. Totally blew his parents' practical family station wagon out of the water. He raised his head to celebrate his release.

Grinning as they slowed for a red light, he saw a fit-looking man admire the car while waiting for the pedestrian crossing. That was the physique Blaine had always imagined himself having. Though his own build was smaller and much leaner, he was certain a few months of gym work could yield some noteworthy results.

Maybe enough to make Sophie look twice …

The man's focus shifted from the car to the pretty blonde driver. Then he spotted Blaine's matted head of half-hearted curls poking out the back. For an instant their eyes met. Blaine saw the narrowing of the man's gaze and then the sudden glare of white as his eyes popped round, like ping-pong balls with dots.

It was like a dream in slow motion. The lights changed and the car accelerated. The man ran after them, shouting. Blaine ducked down in case the driver caught him in her rear vision mirror. And she'd be likely to look, especially with some crazed gym junkie running after her, screaming for her to stop.

Surely it didn't seem *that* strange to have a dirty adolescent in the back of a sports car?

Blaine hunched back down and turned onto his back. It was a bit awkward, but it felt incredible to feel the wind in his face and watch the sky. Too-loud music pounded through his body as the vehicle sped along the freeway. Blaine had no idea where they were going, but he was out! Free to return to his parents, *free to—*

He stopped. Dr Hartfield had said they'd been building a profile of his life for the past three years. He had to think differently; do things he'd never normally do. Besides, what would Dr Hartfield tell his parents and who would they believe?

No, it was not yet safe for him to go home.

Without his mobile phone and wallet, Blaine knew he'd also have to find cash. *Fast.* Most of all, he had to find a way to contact his mum without getting nabbed by the Hartfield rat-pack. It was imperative he acquire a sufficient supply of Ramer's Cure before his emergency stock ran out.

CHAPTER 12

Eddie was sure his heart had nearly blown out of his chest. He had sprinted all the way back to the institute, only to realise the network was still down and he couldn't get through the secured external doors. *Can get out, but not in ...* Demanding action of the car park guards, he was reluctantly provided a master key and gained access to the stairwell. Bounding up eight flights of stairs to the lab, he unlocked the door, burst into the corridor and continued to run.

'Mel! He's gone.' Throwing open the door to her office, he watched her freeze. Her eyes were huge—probably as round as his were when he'd seen Blaine Colton sitting in the back of that sports car. 'Blaine's gone.'

Her mouth opened and closed several times, but she didn't act. In the end, he strode across her office and grabbed her arm to lift her from her chair. His sweaty palm felt clammy against her elbow.

She pulled back violently. Eddie was sure she'd all but ripped her arm from its socket. 'Don't touch me, Eddie.' She followed him out the door, towards the observation room. 'How could he have possibly gotten out on full surveillance?'

'Dunno.'

'Eddie, you'd better not be pulling some stunt to get yourself attention.'

Eddie pivoted to an immediate stop, impatient with her insinuations. It wasn't the first time. 'Mel, I saw him in the back of a red convertible. I swear.'

Her whole face dropped. She grabbed his arm, propelled herself around him, and ran the remaining length of the corridor. By the time he caught up, she was frantically swiping her card up and down the reader on the external door of the observation room.

'Network's down. Can get out without swipe access, but you can't get in.'

Melissa glared at him, raged out loud and then kicked the door hard. 'Well, how did he get out the other side?'

Eddie shrugged, enjoying her tantrum. It was a rare moment the carefully constructed Dr Hartfield completely lost it. 'What now, Mel?'

'Well, if that woman stops ringing me, I'll be able to think!'

Belinda Colton. 'At least now you'll not have the guilt of lying about Blaine being on his way home. Could even 'fess up about your fictitious "the regulating body wants you" claims you made to Blaine at the same time.'

Melissa thumped him on the shoulder. 'Oh, shut up.' She turned and stalked back to her office.

Blaine decided he'd had enough of joy-riding. When they pulled up at an intersection, he jumped out of the car and bolted through the congested traffic before the red light turned green.

The driver must have caught sight of him in her rear vision mirror. She twisted in her seat, evidently bumping the accelerator with her foot and nearly crashing into the vehicle in front. The last thing Blaine saw as he darted around a corner was her look of relief as she held up a wallet.

The city. He ran into an arcade and followed it through to the Queen Street Mall. People jostled past like a surging river of bodies. He caught a flash of blue and the familiar profile of police officers on patrol.

Glancing about, he noticed several surveillance cameras. In the Mall there were many more—*and probably even facial recognition software as well.* 'Time to make myself scarce.'

Pulling the hood of his jacket up over his head, he set out along Albert Street, towards the Botanic Gardens. Blaine figured there would be a little more privacy there. Perhaps he could even hide at the adjoining university campus—at least until the buzz of his escape died down.

Blaine crossed Alice Street into the gardens, leaving behind the chessboard of faceless skyscrapers, fancy hotels, cafés and businesses dominating the CBD. His stomach growled and soon began wrestling itself, reminding him it was lunchtime.

At least they'd given him decent food during his confinement. He'd miss that, if nothing else.

A more pressing concern than lunch was that he only had one more dose of Ramer's Cure. Two tablets in over a week weren't going to sustain him for long. It would be sensible to take a third before his health slipped further. But if he wasn't gaining access to more medication immediately, he knew he should wait.

He wasn't feeling bad yet, and figured some Cure when he needed it might tide him over better than none. He decided to break the single tablet in half. *If I only use one half every second day, I might almost make a week. So long as I can cope with the temperature spikes and associated weakness as the levels in my system drop.* Just when that might happen was unknown.

Blaine took a deep breath and pulled out the clear clip-seal bag holding the remaining dose. Gripping the Ramer's Cure tablet within the plastic, he snapped it in two between his fingers. He held the tiny bag up to his eye. It wasn't a particularly even break, and part of the tablet had broken away in a third granule-like fragment.

He shoved the bag with the pieces of Cure back in his pocket, ready for when he needed it. Of utmost importance was remaining unpredictable. He had to keep his pursuers guessing.

Ambling across the close-cut lawn, Blaine followed one of the paths. A dapple of sunlight flickered on the pavement as he walked past clumps of tall bamboo. His feet began to feel like dead weights. *Surely my body isn't going downhill already?*

He walked a little more, ensuring he changed direction and crossed his own path several times. Eventually he eased himself onto the grass near the ornamental ponds. He felt okay but didn't want to risk a seizure by not resting.

Then there'll be no hope of escape if Vampire Hartfield finds me. With his head cushioned by his folded arms, he allowed sleep to claim him.

Sun warmed Blaine's body like a heavy quilt. He scrubbed at his eyes and pushed himself into a sitting position. The shade he'd been lying under had shifted and he was exposed to direct sunlight.

His stomach yowled. Blaine decided to head for the university, ensuring he took the long way around. He figured it couldn't be much after midday and maybe he'd get lucky with some food.

Going riverside, he passed an assortment of boats moored along the bank. A constant stream of sweat-slicked runners came from both directions. Blaine was forced to walk on the left to allow them an unobstructed path. Soon a group of students passed him, laughing and chatting about lecture schedules and student activities. He followed them a short distance to the Queensland University of Technology.

As he explored the campus referred to as 'Gardens Point', a picture of the fit guy who had run after the car kept plonking itself into his mind's eye. It was like his brain was trying to tell him something important.

Blaine was unsure of what to do next. He decided the best way to get food was to make friends or join in any activities going on. He soon realised he'd picked a good day for it. Semester Two had only just begun and the campus was a hive of activity.

He managed to score hot dogs from a Student Life group. Most of the others asked for a gold coin donation, but this group apparently felt generous—either that or he looked as hungry as he felt and they took pity on him. They even let him come back for seconds and thirds.

After collecting his last serving, he found himself a spot on a grassy expanse across from Old Government House. Before settling on the lawn, he noticed some students were relocating to the gardens. He followed them.

It was best to stay fairly close to a crowd, just in case Hartfield's rat-catchers happened upon him—not that they were likely to find him at an inner-city university campus.

As he walked, city sounds hummed across the gardens, broken by the occasional honk from the car horn of an impatient driver. Fainter, but still audible through the discordant melee, were the steady engines of watercraft on the river.

Blaine knew he stank. Even though it was winter, the Queensland sun shone brightly and he'd worked up a sweat when escaping. This was made worse by the musty smell of his unlaundered clothes and the fact it had been over twenty-four hours since he'd last showered. It hadn't occurred to him to request deodorant while being held at ARI.

As he settled onto the grass near a large fig tree, he heard a rustling in the nearby shrubbery. In a blink, a large brown rat darted out from under a bush, paused with a quiver, and then disappeared into the undergrowth further along.

'Yeah, I'd run too, rodent. Gettin' a bit on the nose out here.'

Blaine sniffed at his shirt. It wasn't dreadful—but it wasn't great either. 'A definite Le Rêve reject.' He wondered if he should try to beg some coins and get another set of clothes. *But I don't want to draw attention to myself. Maybe there're some showers I could use at the uni. Or I could duck across the river to South Bank Parklands and use the showers there.* The only downer was the lack of hot water, hardly an enticing prospect mid-winter.

As Blaine chewed into the soft bread and barbequed sausage, sauce squelched out the other end. It stained the disposable napkin wrapped around the roll and spilled onto his fingers.

Now, he not only smelled homeless, but he also sported food smears and sticky fingers. Good thing there was no one to impress.

CHAPTER 13

'Blaine?'

Blaine nearly choked on the chunk of bread he'd just shoved into his mouth. Thumping his chest, he managed to get the last portion of hotdog down.

Tilting back his head, he found himself looking up into a familiar face framed by a mass of long, light brown ringlets. Full pink lips parted in a friendly smile.

'Blaine, it *is* you.'

'Sophie? What are you doing here?'

'I'm at QUT, remember? Do you mind if I join you? I've only seen you for, like, two seconds since New Year.'

Blaine did remember Sophie's acceptance into a science degree, but had forgotten which university it was. He was suddenly conscious he had sauce all over his face. As he wiped the napkin over his hands and mouth, he noticed some slight blemishes in her complexion. He'd had a few outbreaks of his own recently. He ruffled his hair and hoped he didn't look too bad.

Sophie settled onto the grass beside him. She'd only mentioned it in passing, but Blaine's memories of New Year's Eve overran every other thought. 'That was a great night.'

'New Year's Eve?' At his nod, a light flush coloured her

cheeks. 'Yeah. One of the best of my life. And not just because it was my eighteenth birthday next day.' Her dimples appeared. 'And Jett's, too. Remember?'

Blaine thought he'd never forget. New Year's Eve celebrations with the Coltons and the Faradays were an annual tradition. They'd gather at South Bank to see the New Year in and watch the fireworks displays and festivity. The crowds were tightly-packed, making it difficult to move, especially with a wheelchair in tow. Blaine knew how often this had restricted their outings. But last year he hadn't needed a mobility aid.

He'd joined a spontaneous street dance party with Sophie and her twin brother Jett. They'd stayed up most of the night dancing and singing—not that he could do either well. Their parents had gone home, leaving them to stay to watch the sunrise, ride The Wheel of Brisbane and hang out at Streets Beach.

His heart sang as he watched his parents leave. Other than time spent in needs-specific care facilities, he'd never been out of their sight since they'd adopted him. Of all the many gifts they had given, trusting him with his own freedom was close to the top.

Afterwards, he'd caught the train home with Sophie and Jett to prepare for their birthday party that evening.

Sophie nudged him with her elbow, breaking into his thoughts. 'Bet you can't top that for *your* eighteenth.'

Blaine shrugged and tried to reduce his grin, but it refused to leave his face. 'You never know. I've always fancied a sunrise balloon ride—or even a group skydiving jump.'

She laughed. 'It's only weeks away and I've not got any invitation from you. You'd best get planning.'

Blaine watched the sparkle in her eyes. They reminded him of a curious kitten. The prettiest shade of green, they were forever seeking out information and searching for fun. Growing up, he had always enjoyed it when Sophie and Jett came to their house.

He realised it was probably hugely tedious for them before his treatment. Even so, they had included him in conversation, taken him to the park in his wheelchair and, even in the years before he'd spoken a properly formed syllable, treated him as if he were a fully-able, mentally-equal peer. At times they'd bring their baby sister, Anna, to play. But sitting with a boy in a chair usually proved too much for the small girl's patience.

Then, when he could express himself clearly and move independently, they'd moved way out to Wynnum. Blaine got himself a social media account the same day. Sophie and Jett were the first two friends he connected with.

Sophie frowned. 'I didn't know you were at uni. Did you get accepted for a second semester intake?'

Blaine forced his eyes to the grass. He plucked a few leaves, rolled them between his fingers. 'Nah.' He glanced at her and reminded himself it was impolite to stare. He looked away. 'I'm just checking it out. Wasn't eligible for tertiary entrance with my pointless academic record, remember? But I'm thinking I'd like to do something next year, if I can get in under exceptional circumstances or something.'

'Oh.' She shrugged. 'I was hoping I might get to see you more. How'd we ever get so busy we haven't caught up properly in over six months? I miss hanging out.'

Blaine shrugged back and tried not to read too much into her claim. Sophie and Jett had always been kind to him. Yet he'd also wondered how they'd suddenly found themselves largely out of touch in a matter of months.

Even after the Faradays had moved, their parents had made the effort to organise frequent family visits. In fact, after finishing high school last year, Blaine saw Sophie and Jett nearly every weekend, and often at South Bank. That was, until after New Year's Day. *Did what happened that day change things too much? Or did Sophie and Jett feel released from their obligations to me?*

Life was busy. That was a fact. In honest moments, Blaine suspected it was a relief for them to not have to sit with him for hours on end. Even when he'd undergone Professor Ramer's therapy, it was a long time before he made significant progress with his physical movement. It would have been more than a little frustrating waiting for him to do something the average Jack could manage without thought. Speech had come easier, being something he could practice independently. At least they could talk. Even so, his rehab had been painfully slow. *Yet Sophie sounded so genuine just then* ...

He tried to gauge her expression. 'What's Jett up to? Hasn't messaged me for a couple of months and puts hardly anything on social media these days.'

'Got his apprenticeship as a fitter and turner. Has been crazy busy since starting. Figures he can make a packet in the mines once he's done.'

'And you're still happy doing science?'

Sophie's eyes grew even brighter. To Blaine this seemed impossible and an entire series of 'do not stare' reminders beeped inside his head. He ignored them.

'I am *totally* loving my first year of biomed. You should come to some of my lectures. You'd like it, especially having had firsthand experience. In fact ...' She paused, her eyes growing even more animated. They were almost glowing as she leaned towards him. 'You should come tomorrow. We've got guest lecturers to kick off the semester. Apparently they've been associated with National Science and Engineering Week activities for a couple of years now.

Since that usually coincides with the initial weeks of semester two, this year our course academic invited them to address our class. They're talking about gene therapy.'

Reminded of his predicament, Blaine realised how close she was sitting and how badly he stank. He remembered he could also be putting her in danger.

He scrambled to his feet. 'I—I've got to get going, Sophie. It was great seeing you.'

She looked at him and also stood. A small crease furrowed her brow and she inclined her head towards him. 'Well ... yeah, it was great seeing you too.'

Blaine found his mind blank.

She shrugged. 'If you do want to come tomorrow, the lecture's at 1 pm.' She hesitated before giving him the room number.

'Thanks, Sophie, I've ... I've lost my phone. Would you mind ...?' He stopped and reminded himself that contacting his parents was exactly what Hartfield's hounds would expect him to do. Yet he had to let them know something. It was only right.

'Mind what, Blaine?'

'Would you mind messaging my mum for me?'

'Sure. But just call her. I don't mind.' She shoved her phone with its bright purple cover towards him, her smile back in place.

Blaine knew he shouldn't do it, but every part of him ached to see his parents. They were the ones who had seen value in him, even when his birth mother had rejected him. *Well, at least that's what I thought ...*

Tentative, he reached for the iPhone and took it from Sophie's warm fingers. 'Thanks.'

Dialling the number, Blaine was surprised when his mum's number still flashed up in Sophie's contacts. He smiled. He hadn't had a mobile phone when Sophie and Jett's family had moved. In fact, his iPhone was a fairly recent purchase. He'd not been bold enough to offer Sophie his number yet. *Maybe I could add it to her list—if I ever get my phone back.*

The phone rang and rang.

Please pick up, Mum. Please.

Never one to sit on her phone like it was an extra appendage, his mother usually still had it within earshot, unless she was doing a Le Rêve party. Seconds later the call went to message bank and her pre-recorded voice came through the speaker.

Blaine walked a few paces away from Sophie as he listened to the 'please leave a message' spiel. A beep signalled for him to start. 'Hi Mum, it's Blaine. I'm on my way home. I've lost my phone, but I'm okay and I'll be in contact soon. I ... I miss you and Dad heaps. Bye.'

That gravel-like lump he'd contended with days ago returned to his throat. 'Thanks, Soph.' His words were rasped as he handed back the mobile.

'Are you alright? You just seem a bit ... weird ... on edge.'

Blaine pushed his hands in his pockets and shrugged. Looking out across the gardens, he tried to swallow, but he simply couldn't.

'Blaine, do you have any money?'

His eyes shot to Sophie's and he wondered how she'd guessed.

'I think I saw you at the Student Life stand. I hang out with some of those guys. You looked like you hadn't eaten in a while.'

Heat crept up Blaine's neck and face. 'No,' he croaked.

'I can take you home.'

'I can't go home yet.'

'Well, you could come to our house for the night. Jett would love to see you.'

Blaine shook his head, knowing it would only entangle them in his dilemma. Besides his parents, the Faradays were the nicest people he knew. And Sophie, well ... No way was he going to encourage any more interaction than was necessary.

What was 'necessary'? *If only I didn't have this freak genetic disorder ...*

'Where will you spend the night?'

'Huh?' Blaine realised he'd been staring again. 'Oh, tonight? I figured there'd be a 24 hour computer lab on campus, or something. I had a sleep in the gardens before. Should be all right.'

The frown he'd rarely seen on her brow returned. He could see her struggling not to ask what was going on. To let him keep his secrets. She was opening her mouth when he cut in. 'You don't suppose the gym will mind if I borrow their bathrooms for a bit? My manly musk is getting a bit overpowering and I'm hoping I don't need to do a clench-and-chill rinse at South Bank.' He grinned self-consciously and scuffed his toe across the grass.

'Your "musk" is definitely not great.' Sophie's uneasy smile flashed back. 'I've got a gym pass. Why don't you get freshened up?' She straightened, as if she'd made up her mind. 'Then I'll take you to meet some friends of mine. Our next lecture is in a couple of hours. We've booked a room at the library to do some work on a group assignment until then. You can help us. It's on genetic technologies.'

Her sudden laugh was contagious. Blaine smiled as she grabbed his hand and led the way. *So much for not encouraging unnecessary interaction.*

CHAPTER 14

'Mrs Colton, what a surprise to hear from you.'

'Blaine left a message yesterday to say he was on his way home, but he's still not back.'

'Mrs Colton, I don't mean to alarm you, but the last time I saw Blaine he was not very rational. It seemed the treatment was starting to affect his mental stability.'

'But he was fine when he left here a little more than a week ago for your unscheduled appointment.'

Melissa stared; her mind lost for a moment.

'Dr Hartfield?'

'I'm sorry, I was just thinking that with his condition deteriorating quickly, along with the shock of the poor report ... well, a lot can happen in a week.'

'It's unlike him. Hopefully he'll turn up soon, though I don't know how he'll get on now he's out of your care.'

'I'm sure he'll be fine.'

'But he only keeps a few back-up pills of Ramer's Cure on him. That is, unless he was supplied more when you realised the records were wrong?'

Melissa's mouth twisted. Through clenched teeth she said, 'No, we didn't. It would have been unnecessary, given he was heading home. But he should still have his back-up supply. I'll let you know if we hear anything. Good day, Mrs Colton.'

Melissa hung up the receiver and noticed Eddie draped against the frame of her open door. His arms were folded loosely across his chest, and he sported a measured smile that made her intestines form tight knots.

'Difficulties, Mel?'

She stabbed him with a glare and tapped the end of her pen on her notepad in a rapid staccato. Stopping abruptly, she curled her fingers into a fist and glared at the man crowding her doorway. 'It seems that young Mr Colton was holding out on us.'

'Oh?' Eddie's brow rose.

'He had an emergency supply of Ramer's Cure, as they call it.' She thumped her fist against the desk, irked by the fact Ramer, in electing to name the medication after himself, managed to spruik about his achievements without even being present. 'Several days' worth—however many that is.'

'He obviously didn't use it.'

Melissa's whole body slumped and she pulled a face at him. 'You don't think that could have been something to do with the fact he needed to save them for his escape?'

'But to nearly kill himself for it?'

'Wouldn't *you* if you faced a life imprisoned as an illegal GMO?'

'Illegal GMO?' Eddie rolled his eyes. 'Where do you come up with these notions, Mel?'

Melissa swivelled her chair around to study the lab scene behind them. 'He didn't trust me. Surely one of *them* must have helped him.' She whipped back around. 'I want *every* millisecond of surveillance camera feed from yesterday scrutinised.'

'Except the cameras were out for that hour when the network went down.'

Melissa's head snapped up. Her eyes locked on his face. 'What?'

'It's all networked with this new system, remember? They're trying to change the set-up, but currently when the network goes down, so do the phones, several instruments, and the security feed.'

'And the swipe card recognition ...' She frowned. 'He must have forced the locks.'

'It's possible with a card. I think he used that Monopoly card on the floor.'

Melissa slid her biro into her pen holder. 'One thing I know for sure; that kid's much smarter than any records indicate. He's supposed to have a mental age of a seven-year old.'

Eddie snorted. 'Mel, you didn't trust the *records* over his *obvious* intelligence?'

She refused to answer.

Eddie laughed. 'Another thing we know, my lovely, is he's already used one or two tablets. That means he's going to be in contact with mummy pretty fast.'

'I've already got Sam watching the house, but we need to get someone onto Blaine's profile to determine what his next likely move will be. Although, if he's as smart as we now think, I might've blown that during the consultation.' Melissa watched Eddie's eyebrows rise and answered his unspoken query. 'I said we'd been monitoring him since his treatment.'

'Is that true?'

Melissa turned back to the glass and stood up. She focussed on a research assistant loading small tubes into a microcentrifuge and shrugged. 'Yeah, once his astonishing improvement was public, I made sure he was monitored. You know, Eddie ...' She glanced over her shoulder. '… social media, banking, GPS tracking—that sort of thing.'

'*What?*'

'There needed to be some accountability. Especially after Ramer dropped off the planet.'

'Dropped off the planet? Didn't you tell me Ramer's signature comes back on each copy of those reports?'

Melissa snorted, but otherwise ignored him. No way was she giving Eddie any clue as to how much those signatures haunted her. Ramer had, as always, gotten things his way at her professional expense. And now he seemed untouchable.

'That's it. I'm out.'

She was surprised by Eddie's sudden change of tone. 'What?' She turned so fast she nearly toppled against her chair.

His face was serious, all mocking laughter gone. 'It's gone too far, Mel. I don't even *want* to know how you accessed that information. It's getting too complicated. You can't do that *and* then tell him. I never wanted to do this in the first place, and you know it.'

She felt her brow wrinkle like unpressed linen. 'No way. You don't back out now. Besides, Blaine won't know I was stretching the bounds of his agreement. It was the best way to convince him of his potential danger to society without blowing the lid on the whole ethics and adverse events problem created by Ramer's lack of cooperation.'

Eddie's smile was thin. He looked like a petulant child challenging a figure of authority. 'You think Blaine Colton's going to take this lying down? He's proven he's no fool. And you've got nothing to hold me, *Dr* Hartfield.'

'Grants?' She arched a brow to back her threat. 'Can't do much research without money.'

Eddie folded his arms and chuckled. 'It's not that important to me. Besides, it was *you* who had to know what Ramer did. *You* who had to pull the illegal GMO thing. I'm not buying your excuses anymore. It doesn't add up.' He looked her right in the eye, as if daring her to stop him. 'Why couldn't you just leave the kid alone?'

Melissa felt like she'd touched a live electrical wire. He'd figured it out. There was no point pretending. 'And always be the "me too" scientist? *Always* the one on Ramer's heels with my research echoing *his* achievements?'

'Well, you can do it *without* me.'

Time to employ all out blackmail. She *needed* his expertise. 'I'll pull your funding *and* report that little incident you had in the lab with that modified herpes virus last year.' Melissa folded her arms to mirror him, certain he'd change his mind.

Eddie smirked. 'Incident *I* had?'

'Well, it all depends on how the report is worded, wouldn't you say?'

His lips retreated to a tight line. 'Shall we call the committee, then? I'm certain they already smell a rat—and I don't mean the ones that squeak. And if they don't, just wait until the PI gets back.' He stepped towards her desk and picked up her handset. The dial tone hummed between them.

'If I go down, so do you.' Through narrowed eyes she tried to read his expression, wondering if she should have been looking closer to home for the suspect who'd helped Blaine escape. 'You wouldn't *dare*, Eddie.'

It was several seconds before he spoke. 'Had you going, didn't I?' The smirk stretched back into place as he hung up the phone.

She slumped back into her seat. 'Eddie, you're despicable.'

He laughed, but the tenor was wooden. 'You should've seen the look on your face. I'll take you out to dinner to make it up to you.'

She wanted to thump him. No way would she reward him for threatening her. *Perhaps he's just testing the waters, though.* She made a mental note to limit the amount of critical information she shared with him, although it was a bit late for that.

'And Mel, don't forget we've got that presentation at one. I'll drive.'

She groaned. 'Fine. I'll see you then.'

CHAPTER 15

Tension streamed from Blaine's body as water pulsed against his skin. Yesterday Sophie had obtained a two-day gym guest pass for him. It had been easy. The gym was offering guest trials to entice students to sample their fitness equipment—and hopefully take out membership.

Lathered, scrubbed and clean, he reached to turn off the tap when he realised it wasn't just the water temperature making him hot. He needed more Ramer's Cure than he was getting. A wave of weakness washed through him and his legs buckled. Sliding down the shower cubicle wall, he struggled for breath. The water hitting his skin burned like tiny, smouldering coals, as if every nerve ending was on fire. He struggled to remain alert as the fever throttled his strength. It didn't help that he hadn't eaten since the previous night.

Finally it began to subside. With the worst over, he clawed up the wall to gain his feet and turned off the tap. Reaching for his towel, he shambled out of the cubicle. Sinking onto a nearby bench, he rested the back of his head against the wall. The cement was a cold patch of relief against his heat-scorched skin.

Why the fevers?

Even in that special meeting his parents had demanded with "someone more appropriately qualified", Professor Ramer hadn't been able to fully explain why his body temperature would intermittently spike following his treatment. Dr Hartfield's claim he could have been infected with a disease seemed reasonable, but this had never been suggested before in any of his follow-up assessments. He'd been concerned, but the spikes had been so rare ... then. Now, even when he took Ramer's cure, he'd experience a rapid increase in body temperature nearly once a week. If he forgot his medication for any notable period, he risked a seizure.

Are the two connected? And why are the fever spikes increasing?

Other gym-goers passed him on their way to and from workouts. Some people asked if he was all right. Blaine used the excuse he'd overdone it on his first day, and assured them he'd be fine in a minute. While resting, he thought about the previous afternoon.

He'd spent the time with Sophie and her friends. She'd told them about his brush with gene therapy and he'd achieved automatic hero status. They'd visited the Science and Engineering Centre and played with 'The Cube', a large multi-sided interactive learning display sporting two life-sized virtual simulations. It was cool prodding the interactive touch screen to explore features of various reef sea creatures, the theme on one side. When he got bored, he went to play with the anti-gravity animations on the other.

Later, he'd sat in on a lecture on human health and disease. It was interesting. Better than sitting in a white, fluoro-lit holding cell. Even spending the night in a computer lab hadn't been so bad—much warmer than a bench at South Bank or somewhere.

Eventually Blaine was able to dress. He tried not to inhale as he pulled his shirt over his head. *I so need another set of clothes.* The soft material rasped against his chin. He glanced in the mirror to check his beard wasn't too scrappy. All over, he was beginning to look like a cover model for a homelessness awareness campaign.

He took one half of a Ramer's Cure. Hopefully it would ease

his symptoms for at least another day.

Exiting the gym, Blaine caught sight of a clock. He was late.

Sophie had arranged to meet him at 12:50pm, but it was already 12:55pm. He covered the short distance to the building where the lecture was being held, jogged up the stairs, and slipped in through a double door side entrance.

He saw her wave as he entered the lecture theatre, then recognised some faces from yesterday. They were sitting three rows from the front, near the centre aisle.

'Hey, Blaine, you're late. Maybe you should've taken a taxi. Must be slowing up in your old age.'

Blaine grinned and shook his head. Sophie grinned back. She had already insisted on giving him a handful of coins. He knew she was torn over how to best help him. At least she'd promised not to tell his parents where he was, until he agreed she could.

'Soph, I only used a few dollars last night to get something from a campus café. You can have the rest of your money back, if you want.'

'No, silly, I said to keep it.' She shoved his arm and rolled her eyes. 'Oh, and I got this for you. Well, I swiped it from Jett's room. He had a spare.'

Blaine nudged her back as she handed him a calico bag. Peering inside, he saw a can of deodorant. They looked each other in the eye, until Sophie seemed to realise they were both staring. She broke eye contact and reached again into her backpack.

'Oh, your mum called about an hour ago. Well ...' She pulled a face he couldn't quite interpret. '... she'd actually called a few times before then, but my phone was charging and I didn't hear it. Anyway, I told her I was seeing you today and promised I'd get you to call her back.'

She'd handed Blaine the phone, when they were interrupted by a microphone test. He turned his attention to the front—and saw gym guy!

It's the guy whose eyes made ping-pong balls when he saw me in the back of the red convertible.

'Blaine, are you okay? You look like you've been bleached.'

Blaine nodded and tried to smile. He realised gym guy hadn't seen him. The man was looking at some girls making flirtatious remarks near the front. He said something in response that Blaine couldn't hear, but when the girls giggled, the dots connected.

I recognise that hair. And eyes. Eddie. Gym guy was one of the coats who had peered at him over a surgical mask, through a plastic shield.

Skulking down in his seat, Blaine glanced across the full theatre. There were students everywhere.

What are the chances he'll see me?

'Sophie …' Blaine passed her phone back, his voice a low whisper. 'I … I have to go.'

'What?'

'I have to—'

The buzz in the theatre fell away to silence as the guests were introduced. '... Dr Edward Jonick, staff scientist at Advance Research Institute, or ARI as it is known, and the institute's Director and Chief Scientist, Dr Melissa Hartfield.'

Um, God, if you're there and listening, I might need some help right about now.

The lecturer extended his hand towards the rear of the theatre and all eyes turned. Blaine slunk down further and glanced over his shoulder. On the centre aisle at the back of the room was Dr Hartfield. She gave a small wave.

I'm doomed.

He hoped, *prayed*, they wouldn't see him in the large group of students. Though he had no pen or paper, he kept his head down and strove to look like an excessive note-taker.

Blaine felt like someone had sucked the air out of the room. His chest hurt and his hands grew numb. Over and again he rehearsed his options in his head, but there was no way out now.

'Blaine, what's up?'

Only then did he realise how closely Sophie was watching him. *Gotta pull it together.* 'I'm good,' he whispered, forcing himself to inhale and exhale in deep, regular, cycles.

Dr Jonick's voice stopped being a low, distracting, jumble. Words began to seep in and make sense. Although commercial-in-confidence agreements limited some details being given, Dr Jonick covered the principles behind their research and its ultimate application in the treatment of genetic disorders. To Blaine's surprise, he found the talk interesting.

Rounding up, Dr Jonick introduced Dr Hartfield. Blaine felt more than heard her descend the centre aisle. *Talk about making an entrance.* His seat was just two in from the central throughway, and he felt like a mouse forced into a loaded trap. She could just lean over and grab him by the collar if she knew he was there.

His breath burst from his mouth when she reached the front. Dr Jonick took a seat in the first row and Blaine realised there was a clear path to the rear exit. Granted, he was closer to the front than the back, but even if they saw him, what were they going to do in front of all the other students? All he had to do now was sit inconspicuously and he would simply leave with his friend.

Dr Hartfield talked on about the group's research, their achievements and future directions. She also promoted the potential opportunities the institute presented in the way of post-graduate and post-doctoral positions, along with summer scholarships for undergraduate students.

With just five minutes to go, Blaine relaxed. He was so far out of context. Even if they saw him, he was certain neither Dr Hartfield nor Dr Jonick would recognise him before he had time to run.

Dr Hartfield had just begun her summary when he saw her eyes grow round. She stumbled over her words and he had to check twice to ensure she wasn't looking at him.

There was someone at the back putting her off.

Blaine twisted in his seat to take a glance over his shoulder. There, blocking the rear exit was a man Melissa clearly recognised.

Should I run now, while she's distracted? Is he connected to ARI?

Caught between the fear of betraying his presence and his desperation to escape, Blaine was momentarily paralysed. Before he'd settled on an action, he noticed Dr Jonick had moved to the side of the auditorium and was making his way to the rear exit, where the other man stood. His movement seemed to have escaped most of the attendees—except those girls up front who still giggled as they tracked his progress.

Blaine's whole strategy had to be reconsidered.

With his heart surging like a firefighting water pump, Blaine felt dots of sweat break out on his skin. Now that Dr Jonick was with the man at the back, he'd somehow have to make it to the side exit—without being seen by either ARI representative.

Returning his attention to the front, Blaine was just in time to hear Dr Hartfield mention their work with mitochondrial disease. A couple of Sophie's friends jostled each other and murmured approval. From the corner of his eye he caught their attempts to gain his attention, but he ignored them, hoping neither of the guest speakers would notice.

Dr Hartfield completed her address. After answering some questions, the lecture ended. Students ambled from the theatre like cattle in a sorting yard. Blaine glanced about the room, but there was now no sign of the man who had rattled Melissa Hartfield. Both Dr Jonick, still at the back, and Dr Hartfield were surrounded by students. A couple of Sophie's friends had gone to the front to speak further about Dr Hartfield's research, but thankfully Sophie had settled on grabbing a bite to eat before going with him to the gardens.

Blaine inched along behind her. They were hemmed in, with students streaming out of their seats causing a major bottle neck at the side exit as bodies poured from the long rows.

'Let's go out the back way, Blaine.'

He didn't move. 'No, the side's easier.'

She frowned at him. 'You must like waiting. There's no one behind us.'

Then the unthinkable happened.

A voice rang out. 'Sophie's friend had gene therapy for a mitochondrial disorder—and he's here!'

Blaine heard the words, spoken so loudly they split through the general din of chatter. He glanced in horror as the overeager student pointed him out to Dr Hartfield. There was nothing he could do to hide. Every eye in the place had fallen on him.

Blaine saw Melissa Hartfield look to her colleague. Immediately Dr Jonick was at the end of the row, blocking the aisle. He began striding towards Blaine.

Blaine looked around. There were students in every direction, except between him and Dr Jonick, who was just metres away. He glanced forward and saw Dr Hartfield had moved to the opposite end of the row.

His breathing and heart rate raced each other, making him light-headed. He was trapped. 'Sorry, Soph, I've got to go.'

'Just wait, silly.'

But there could be no waiting. Blaine got up on the table behind them and jumped from one row to the next, narrowly escaping Dr Jonick's grasp. He heard the coat curse as he jostled his way through objecting clumps of students, but he wasn't stopping for anybody.

CHAPTER 16

Blaine bolted down two flights of stairs and emerged from the building as if leading an invisible stampede. Outside, he hurried away towards more steps, with the aim of losing the coats in the Botanic Gardens. Ascending the stairs two at a time, he continued looking over his shoulder to ensure he wasn't being followed—and collided smack into someone, nearly tumbling backwards with the force.

'Sorry.'

A hand shot out, grabbing Blaine's arm to prevent him falling. Without really looking at the man, he tried to dodge away, his focus locked on the exit from where Drs Hartfield and Jonick would soon emerge. But the hand held firm.

'Blaine? Blaine Colton?'

Blaine whipped around and recognised the guy who had put Melissa Hartfield off during the lecture.

'Wow! Professor Ramer said he'd seen you, that you were doing well, but *look* at you. You're ... you're *running*. From the media coverage alone, I can tell you've grown—a heap.'

Blaine was puzzled by the guy's enthusiasm. 'Dude, who are you?'

The guy stopped gawking and offered his hand. 'Luke Kastenholz. I was part of the research team that developed your gene therapy.' His eyes remained locked on Blaine's face. 'You never saw me, but I saw you—well, your results—many times as our group reviewed your progress and tracked you through the stages of therapy and the first six months of your recovery—until I left. Of course, you were a coded study participant, but it wasn't hard to join the dots once news got out.'

This is a dream. Someone who knows Professor Ramer. 'Did you know the approval wasn't right?'

A deep frown furrowed Luke's brow. 'I didn't look after the approvals, Professor Ramer did. What do you mean by "not right"?' He followed the line of Blaine's darting eyes and looked back towards the building from where they'd both come. 'Are you okay?'

'Dr Hartfield says there's a problem with the therapy.' As soon as Blaine mentioned Melissa Hartfield, he saw Luke tense.

'Dr *Hartfield?*' His tone grew clipped and he clasped Blaine's shoulder, as if it unsettled by the gravity of his words. 'What sort of problem?'

'She said it's failing and—' Movement caught Blaine's eye. He wrenched away from Luke's hold and stumbled up a couple more steps. 'I've got to go.'

Luke glanced from Blaine to the building exit where Dr Hartfield's silhouette was becoming clearer behind the glass of the main door. 'Blaine, wait.'

But Blaine ignored the plea and kept moving. There wasn't a chance he was going to just stand around while Melissa Hartfield snapped a collar on him and dragged him back to his kennel like a runaway dog.

By the time he'd reached the Botanic Gardens, Blaine was exhausted. He knew then he'd seriously underestimated the impact of his reduced dosage of Ramer's Cure. Going to the toilets nearer the centre of the grounds, he hunched down behind them to catch his breath. He was afraid for Sophie. It was highly likely Dr Hartfield had recognised her as the girl on his phone.

He only had half a dose of Ramer's Cure left and already his body was starting to weaken. There was no help for it; he had to get in contact with his mother soon. But Melissa Hartfield and her associates would be waiting for him to do just that. Determined to hold off for another day, at least, he had to stay away for as long as he could.

'Blaine!'

Blaine peeped around the wall of the ablution block. It was Sophie. Dr Jonick and Dr Hartfield were with her. Whatever they'd told her, it seemed she now believed it important for him to be found.

He ducked back behind the toilets and tried to work out a plan. It couldn't involve too much running or he'd be caught for sure. Blaine glanced towards the Alice Street exit. Maybe he should take Sophie's suggestion and catch a cab, only he was pretty sure his limited cash wouldn't even take him one hundred metres.

Time to lose the white coats ...

He moved away from the toilets. Of course they would think of looking there. How could he have been so stupid?

Ensuring the toilets blocked their view, he headed for the northern boundary of the gardens, eventually finding himself on the river. *But what now?*

Deciding the cycle path was too exposed, he walked the periphery of the gardens until he reached a loop to the footbridge that crossed to the southern bank of the river. He wished he could cut back through the campus to intercept Sophie, but it was too risky with the coats hanging around. With a glance at the taller university buildings peering over the tree line, he set off towards South Bank Parklands.

Initially he kept up a brisk pace, but the slight rise in the bridge felt like a climb up Mount Everest. It was tempting to collapse on a bench and sleep for hours. Instead, he pushed on until he was following the wide path through The Arbour at South Bank.

It was there he stopped to rest. Although it was winter, the bright sunshine had brought people out. Some braved the Aquativity playground with their children, a few even paddled at the adjoining Streets Beach. No one paid any attention to him as he lay on a large deck bench to doze in the afternoon sun.

As he got settled, Blaine noticed an ice cream cart beachside. The attendant wasn't doing a great deal of business, though. *Jett would consider that a travesty.*

He smiled. Sophie's twin was addicted. His hankering for ice cream made South Bank a favourite hangout. Besides the Streets ice cream carts, there were New Zealand Natural Ice Cream stands and often a Mr Whippy van. Should they fail, supplies could be obtained from the Cold Rock ice creamery and a number of other nearby cafés.

Jett could go an entire outing eating nothing but ice cream. A chocolate restaurant was more Sophie's style.

The smile tugged at Blaine's mouth further as these thoughts reminded him of his most recent New Year adventure with Sophie and Jett. He drifted off into a pleasant dream he never wanted to end.

CHAPTER 17

'Thanks, Sophie, you've been a great help.'

'Sure. Anything to help Blaine.'

Melissa nodded and glanced at Eddie. 'And he certainly needs it now, with all the trouble he's in. We'll try to get to him before he does anything else irrational. You're lucky he didn't hurt you.' She ignored the scowl that shadowed her colleague's features as she offered this caution.

Sophie folded her arms across her body and brushed her palms against her upper arms. 'I find that hard to believe. It's not like Blaine to do anything violent. He's always been really kind—impulsive maybe, but kind.' Her gaze passed from Melissa to Eddie and back.

'You said it's been a while since you've seen him. Unfortunately the treatment has had unexpected side effects. He's convinced we're trying to hurt him. Whereas we're the only ones who can save him. Paranoia is part of the psychosis and intermittent violence he experiences.' Melissa laced each word with tones of sympathy. 'You've got our mobile numbers. If he contacts you again, let us know immediately. And please, tell his parents you've seen him and also caution them to be careful. We don't want anyone being harmed.'

'Thanks.'

Melissa watched Sophie walk slowly towards Gardens Point campus. She glanced back a couple of times but kept on going.

The girl had said she was heading for the train at South Bank and there was nothing to suggest she had pre-arranged a rendezvous with Blaine. Even so, something deep down inside told Melissa that, if push came to shove, Sophie would opt to defend Blaine Colton every time. From various communications on file, she also had the impression South Bank was a place they liked to hang out together, particularly since his therapy. If hormones and emotions were involved, then even the gravest warning would fall on deaf ears.

'Do you think we've convinced her enough to report any contact with Blaine?'

'We?' Eddie stared hard at her. 'I think she really likes him.'

'And what would *you* know about that, Eddie Jonick?' Melissa glared. 'I saw you flirting with those girls. They're teenagers, for crying out loud. When are you ever going to stop being a jock, get over yourself, and grow up?'

Melissa watched surprise register on Eddie's face. He looked at her for a long time and she wondered if he'd taken her reprimand as interest. Thoughts filtered through her mind and an idea rapidly formed.

Perhaps I could use his interest to my advantage ... 'Say, Eddie, after that show this morning, how about I give you a chance to redeem yourself? You know how you're always asking me out?'

'So?'

'What about South Bank tomorrow night? There are some great new restaurants. I haven't been out in ages.'

'What about Blaine?'

Melissa shrugged. 'He won't go far.' Silently she banked on the predictability of a displaced young man in an upended world finding his way to a familiar location peopled with fond memories.

Light sparked in Eddie's eyes, but his uncertainty at her seriousness was obvious. To seem more authentic, Melissa leaned forward and lifted her hand to place it on his chest. She couldn't quite force herself to complete the action. 'Eddie, I'll give you this—you're persistent, even if you are a jock. Figure it might be time to cut you some slack. In fact, let's go early and make an afternoon of it. We can browse the markets first.'

She pulled back a little too quickly. Having heard Eddie's glorified accounts of his female conquests, she had no intention of being added to the list. But for now, his interest worked to her benefit, and she had to be convincing in her role.

'By the way, what did Kastenholz want? Can't believe the nerve of him turning up at our lecture like that—and then stopping us to ask all those questions when we were following Blaine just now. Nearly blew everything right in front of Sophie.'

He shrugged. 'Completed his PhD and works at the uni now. Heard we'd been invited to do a guest lecture and decided to see where we'd taken our research since he'd left. Don't think anything we said wowed him all that much.'

Melissa gritted her teeth and resisted the desire to thump Eddie hard. Of course Kastenholz would feign disinterest. As if the work he and Ramer's team undertook was superior to her own. 'Let's hope he keeps his mouth shut about Blaine.'

It was then she realised how closely Eddie was studying her. 'What?' But he continued to appraise her with the intensity of someone peering down a microscope. 'He and Ramer get under my skin.' She dared to admit this, simply to distract Eddie's focus, but it didn't seem to even register.

Quit looking at me like that, Eddie.

'I'd think they'd still keep in contact, if Ramer's not dead.'

Eddie blinked and frowned. 'Why would he be dead? That's ridiculous.'

Melissa shrugged. 'Could be. Nothing else really explains his sudden disappearance.'

'He didn't disappear. He resigned from his role at ARI, Mel. You *know* he's not dead. Isn't he allowed to take a better offer from an undisclosed company?'

'With such cryptic forwarding details after the biggest scientific breakthrough of his career?' She shrugged. 'It's just ... bizarre.'

'Anyway, should get going, Mel. Can't keep our car park forever.' For the privilege of their two hour appearance, they had been offered the prized benefit of an on-campus park. Eddie began walking towards the university. He glanced back at her. 'You coming?'

Melissa nearly flinched at the abrupt coolness of his manner. *What's that about?* She was giving him the attention he'd sought for months, and now he was playing hard-to-get? It wasn't like him. But really Eddie was just a means to an end—and it was only the end that mattered.

Eddie was quiet as they drove. He didn't feel like talking and he didn't feel like listening much either. Thoughts ticked through his head as he negotiated the company car through heavy Friday afternoon traffic.

Having advanced no more than fifty metres in five minutes, he glanced again at Melissa. She seemed preoccupied, even agitated.

What she didn't know was, as she'd hastened off to follow Sophie to the gardens, he'd asked Luke about Ramer's contact with Blaine. In those few seconds before Melissa had looked back and clicked her fingers to hurry him along, he'd heard the truth. The contact had been requested through the appropriate channels and approved by the committee as an exceptional safety-determined circumstance, with Ramer being the *only* appropriately qualified person to suitably assess and advise the Colton's on managing Blaine's adverse events. Exceptional. Not illegal. And certainly not a breach of the study agreement.

Melissa was lying through her teeth. Was she also lying about Ramer's lack of cooperation and the supposed non-communications from his group?

What the hell have I got myself tangled up in? And why the sudden show of nice? What does she really *want from me?*

What Melissa also didn't know, and he'd rather hit himself with a brick than admit, was that he was *really* interested in her. Well, he had been. Now that he was getting to know her better, he was discovering a very different side to the enchanting Melissa Hartfield—and he wasn't entirely convinced he liked it.

Fair enough, he did act like a jock and exaggerate the stories about the women he dated. Granted, it was disrespectful. And yes, he did flirt far more than was considered appropriate—although to be fair, those girls in the lecture had been flirting with him, not the other way around. But in rare moments of honest reflection, he knew he did it to cover the fact he'd had his heart ripped from his chest and mashed into a formless lump by the girl he'd thought he'd marry.

Alyce.

If he pretended he didn't care, it actually seemed to keep at bay the dull, permanent ache that had been in his chest for the past five years. *Well, somewhat.*

For that reason he'd been stoked to get the position at ARI, especially after a string of short-term post-doc appointments in

Melbourne. Returning to Queensland meant he'd be near to his family—and far away from Alyce. But his homecoming had not been quite as he'd expected.

He hadn't fit at home anymore, not that he'd wanted to live back with his parents anyway. Then they moved to the Sunshine Coast just after his return. So much for being nearer to them. Even so, the institute had been good for him. *At least it used to be ...*

With another glance at his uncharacteristically silent passenger, he set his jaw. There was no way he was going to let Melissa Hartfield keep using him as a pawn in her increasingly dangerous game of chess. So why did he have the horrid feeling when he looked at her that it was already too late?

CHAPTER 18

Blaine hunched down into his jacket and shivered. A cool breeze crept from the river and harassed him, making it impossible to get warm. Despite the half-portion of Ramer's Cure he'd taken earlier, he was cold yet hot. Even eating the sandwich he'd purchased from a local café had made little difference. Whenever he stood up, he felt dizzy and nauseous. It seemed his condition was growing increasingly unstable.

The sun hung low in the sky and he knew Riverwalk and the bridges would soon light up in brightly-coloured hues. The Wheel of Brisbane would also be illuminated, its huge spokes glowing like part of a giant, iridescent bicycle wheel turning high above the ground.

New Year's Eves of the past ran through his mind. He mentally retraced his steps from that wonderfully mad evening last year with Jett and Sophie. Their laughter rang in his ears; their talk about hopes and dreams echoed in his mind. He could still feel the music that pulsed through the crowd, demanding they move in sync with the rhythm—and Sophie's arms around him as they'd screamed, 'Happy New Year,' so loud it made his throat hurt.

It was the last time he'd hung out with both Sophie and Jett together.

Sophie.

A smile spilled across his mouth. The way she'd grabbed his hand yesterday had reminded him of when they were children. Sophie and Jett had taken him on many walks, one on either side of his chair like a guard of honour. They'd held tightly to his hands as if it was the best thing in the world to know him.

Blaine snorted. 'Best thing—right ...'

Dream on, rat boy. He had to stop thinking about her. It could never be. His genes were messed up. That's what had landed him in this fix in the first place. But of its own accord, his brain returned to their perfect night. *And the amazing day that followed ...*

They had eaten breakfast at a café, taken a bird's eye view of the city through a Wheel of Brisbane gondola—three sweaty, over-excited teenagers amidst the eclectic group of passengers—then ambled about the waterfront. With such a warm day, they had lingered under the arches of the twisted metal pylons lining The Arbour. These ornamental features always reminded Blaine of giant silver leeches. Coiling vines of leafy bougainvilleas snaked about the overhead structures, adding magenta highlights to the greenery.

Jett had, unsurprisingly, decided ice cream would provide the perfect end to their outing. His muscular physique, courtesy of his regular gym attendance, gave no hint of this frequent indulgence. Blaine and Sophie were left alone on a footbridge near the Formal Gardens. It seemed they could never talk enough to make up for the lost years that had held Blaine captive. As he made a joke about something inane, Sophie had grown silent and rested her head against his shoulder.

The booming fireworks that had died away just after midnight seemed to start again within him. Blaine could still remember the warmth of her body as she had leaned into him and tilted up her face. He had never kissed a girl on the lips before and wondered if he even knew how. Somehow, the thought of kissing Sophie had made it seem easy.

Before he could find out, Jett interrupted them with a delivery of soft-serve ice cream in waffle cones.

A ferry pontoon nearby groaned as it rose and fell in the wake of a paddle boat sending waves rolling across the river. The noise made Blaine jump. Another violent shiver rattled through him. Truth was, it was no longer summer and New Year's Day was just a memory.

Blaine had never carried extra weight and now he considered it might have been to his advantage to have a slight amount of insulation. Where could he go to stay warm?

The rest points on Kurilpa Bridge? A train station?

He didn't fancy holing up in a public toilet, but maybe he could wait in the toilets near Streets Beach until they were locked for the night. They had a changing area for swimmers where he could sit comfortably enough. Or perhaps the nearby train station was a better option. Either way, at least it'd be sheltered.

It was then Blaine noticed a familiar figure wandering along the riverside. 'Sophie?'

CHAPTER 19

Sophie wheeled about and froze. 'Blaine?' Her hand dashed into her backpack and snatched out her mobile phone.

Blaine realised what she was doing. 'Please, Sophie, I don't know what they said, but don't call them. *Please.*' He came to his feet and held up his hand.

She looked from the phone to him, her finger poised over the touch screen.

'Please, Soph, don't.'

After a moment, she slipped the phone away. Still, she didn't move nearer him. 'Why are you here, Blaine? Why aren't you at home?'

Blaine buried his hands in his jacket pockets and shrugged. 'You'd think I was crazy if I told you.'

Sophie smiled and his heart thumped double-time in his chest. 'No crazier than usual, Blaine Colton.' She moved towards the bench and sat down on it, patting the space next to her. 'Talk.'

Blaine eased himself down beside her. The last of the day's sunlight peered like fiery embers over the horizon, illuminating Sophie's face in orange hues. Very soon it would be dark. There were enough people about, many attending the Lifestyle Markets that were held each Friday evening, and on Saturdays and Sundays. But for her safety he shouldn't keep her long.

'First, what did Dr Hartfield say to you—other than, I'm guessing, asking you to report my whereabouts?'

Sophie shrugged and scuffed the toe of her shoe against the pavement. 'She said you were really sick, potentially infectious, and ... and you thought they were out to get you.'

'I am and they are—maybe not infectious, but the other things, yeah.'

Her eyes shot up and projected a blend of disbelief and alarm.

'Sophie, I'm not crazy, but I don't know what to do. I don't know who to trust. Dr Hartfield said some stuff ... Stuff about my adoption and Mum and Dad, and them not ...' He shrugged his resignation. 'Apparently there was a problem with the therapy, too. I don't want to put you at risk, so it's probably best we keep this brief.' Blaine wondered if he'd imagined the disappointment in her eyes.

'What will you do?'

'Don't know yet. I have to think things through; try and figure out a way to get the meds I need so I don't end up a waste-of-space vegetable again.'

'Blaine, don't you *dare* say that.'

He didn't look at her. Instead, Blaine pushed himself further back on their seat and fiddled with the zipper of his cargo pocket. 'It's true, Sophie. What good was I?' He turned to study her face and was surprised to see tears pool in her eyes.

'So, you're saying that human life, *your* life, isn't valuable unless it has proven its worth?'

Blaine dropped his head, uncertain what had come over him. He felt angry that his new life was hanging by a thread—unless he wanted to volunteer his existence as an in-house guinea pig for Melissa Hartfield. He was also being forced to run from everyone who meant anything to him, and he wasn't sure he could trust them anyway.

That was no excuse for making Sophie feel lousy.

'Sorry.' He glanced up and felt even more of a heel when one of those tears spilled over and tracked a meandering line down her cheek. 'I just remember so many language-less, drooling, seizure-prone, wheelchair-bound years. You were *so* patient; both you and Jett. I couldn't wait for your visits. You didn't treat me like a charity case or an inconvenience. You made me feel as if I had a right to live, but they were long days, I'm sure.'

Sophie turned to him and looked Blaine right in the eye. 'Then you weren't listening very well, Blaine.'

'Do you mean that time you got all cranky-pants about missing that concert because my chair got stuck in traffic? Or when you and Jett nearly collapsed from exhaustion after pushing me up a rocky incline for two kilometres for the sake of an "easy" scenic walk?' He eyed her impishly.

'Yeah well, maybe you were a pain in the butt at times.' She wrinkled her nose at him. 'But don't forget how often we used to tell you we enjoyed visiting ... *most* days. And we were excited off the chain when you started learning to speak and walk. I couldn't *wait* to hear what you'd *really* been thinking.'

'Not much.' Blaine grinned as she flicked his arm with the back of her fingers.

'You're not funny, Blaine.'

Sophie grew quiet. Drawing her knees up to her chest, she rested her chin on them. Her eyes fixed on a CityCat across the water—the catamaran ferries that operated on Brisbane River.

He studied her, noticing first the way she chewed on the side of her lip, and then the slight pleat of her brow. 'Soph?'

Her eyes swung again to his, conveying her concern with unsettling openness. He knew she deserved an explanation.

'You're right. That was a pretty self-centred little spiel. I just can't imagine it being very fun for you and Jett, when all I could do was ... be. I tried so hard to connect, make proper words, do stuff, but it just came off wrong—or as ... nothing. You can't tell me you weren't ever embarrassed.'

Sophie took a deep breath as her focus drifted back to the water. Letting her knees drop, she momentarily stretched out her legs before tucking them below the bench. 'Yeah, there were times I squirmed and complained, or hid under my hat when we were out. But I still wish you wouldn't say those things, Blaine, or even think them.' She snuck another glance at him. 'Sometimes it was frustrating, but you could be really fun to be with, even when you couldn't respond. Remember us trying to guess what you were thinking?'

'Now *that* was annoying. You and Jett invented the most ridiculous scenarios and there was nothing I could do to object— except muster up an enthusiastic groan.'

'But you'd smile sometimes, even at the silliest jokes, and remind me that life was a gift to make the most out of. You ...'

Blaine watched as she ran her fingers over the bench in the small gap between them.

'You inspired me to do science.' Her face came up, her eyes once again radiating life. 'You were trapped by your failing body, this great listener with a wild sense of humour. I remembered your parents saying you'd developed some language at a toddler age, but as your condition deteriorated it seemed lost forever. I wondered about the things you must have tried so hard to get out.'

'And then once I started again, you couldn't shut me up.' He laughed, parroting what his father frequently said.

Sophie smiled. A faint pink painted her cheeks, adding to the vividness of her features in the shadows of dusk. 'I figured if

I devoted my career to helping someone like you find their voice and live out all those hidden dreams, well, it'd be worth it.'

A warm spot formed somewhere in Blaine's mid-region. He was tempted to reach for Sophie's hand. But he couldn't think straight as she continued to look him right in the eye. All he knew was his stomach was doing gymnastics and he was seriously revisiting that idea of kissing her.

He wasn't quite sure if she took his hand, or he took hers, but somehow they ended up with fingers entwined. Sitting so close, it took only a slight lean for Sophie to have her head against his shoulder with his cheek resting on her hair.

His inner voice shouted at him, telling him he was being hugely unfair; that one day this dream would have to end. But there wasn't a scrap of willpower left in him to act on those sensible statements. *God, if you're really there and you really do care; if there was ever a way for us to ...*

Blaine sighed. For someone who wasn't sure what they believed, he seemed to be making an awful lot of requests of late. Yet, with the wisps of Sophie's hair tickling his face and her fingers curled within his, he could believe just about anything right now. *Could this be some kind sign?*

The moment was shattered by the ringing of Sophie's phone. She pulled away to answer the call, forcing Blaine to let go of her hand.

'Hi, Mum, sorry I didn't call. I bumped into a girlfriend, Sienna, on the way home. She was staying in at uni for a night lecture and then heading out for a bit, so we stopped for a coffee and a bite to eat. Then I saw ...' She smiled at Blaine. '... another friend. Sure, I'm still good for dinner. I'll catch the next train from South Bank. Bye.'

Sophie checked the time on the screen of her phone. 'Blaine,

I've got to rush. That train's due in a few minutes.'

'I'll walk you there.'

'We'll have to run. You up for it?'

Blaine's heart crashed. No, he wasn't. In fact, he was hard pressed maintaining a fast stroll. 'Sorry, Soph, I'll have to pass. I'm not feeling so great right now.'

'Oh ... sure. I understand.' Her voice was flat. She looked up at him after putting her phone in her bag. 'Blaine, I didn't come this way by accident. I was hoping to find you. Please catch the train with me. I'll even call Mum and wait for the next one, then Jett and I can drive you home. Or ring your mum. She could pick you up now.'

'I can't.'

A sigh spilled from her mouth. 'I hate the thought of you being out here all night. You're already cold.'

'It's Brisbane, Soph. Night temps might occasionally drop to single digits, but it's not like it's going to snow.'

'How will I contact you?'

'I'll call—or something. And can you let Mum know I'm okay?'

'Sure. But I still don't understand why you can't just talk to her yourself.'

'Can you also ask her if she knew I was sick before I was adopted?'

Sophie frowned. 'What? Why don't you ask?'

'Please. Ask for me. And I've got to get some meds from her *really* soon—like tomorrow or Sunday, at the latest. Think that's what Dr Hartfield's waiting for me to do. Not sure if she's notified any government organisation or anything. But I can't go back to ARI or I'll never come out alive.'

'Can I get the meds to you?'

'Maybe. Just try and do it on the quiet, or they'll track you down like a pair of hounds.'

'All right, Mr Stubborn. I've got to run.' Still she didn't move, even when they heard the train in the distance. Her eyes begged him to change his mind.

Blaine shook his head and Sophie's shoulders fell. She shrugged on her bag then suddenly straightened, the brightness returning to her face.

'Blaine, I'll get those meds and be back at ten o'clock tomorrow morning. You meet me *right* here, okay?'

'Sophie, I don't—'

'Promise?'

'Okay, promise.' Blaine fidgeted with his thumbnail, struggling to find the right words. 'Soph, you're really great, you know. Thanks.'

She smiled. 'Bye, Blaine. Take care.'

With a quick hug, she was gone. Blaine was suddenly aware of how cold he was.

CHAPTER 20

Blaine decided to head for the South Brisbane train station. It wasn't very far. As he walked, he wondered if he could huddle inside or if there would be a guard on duty to stop him. After all, he didn't have a ticket.

By the time he had covered the short distance, he was shivering so much he could hardly stand. It wasn't just the cool night air, but his body protesting the weakness overriding him. *Maybe I should just take the other half of the Cure.*

As he stepped under the shelter of the building's external awning, strength seemed to leave his legs, forcing him to his knees. The tin of deodorant made a dull clank as the calico bag fell to the ground beside him. Giving up the goal of getting inside, he crawled against the wall, pulled the hood of his jacket over his head and lay on his side. A drunken man was on a seat nearby, raving deliriously to himself.

If only he understood more about why he seemed to improve after resting then, with the slightest exertion, become nearly incapacitated. He got that his cellular powerhouses were failing, but couldn't quite figure out where the temperature spikes fit into the puzzle. Apparently there was still enough Cure in his system to offer limited relief, because he hadn't suffered a seizure since escaping ARI. *But how long will that last with a fragment only every second day?*

'You shouldn't do drugs, kid.'

Blaine lifted his head to find the drunken man leaning over him. He recoiled as a cloud of foul breath wheezed into his face. The man's bloodshot eyes seemed to sink back in his sallow face as he reached down and tugged on Blaine's arm.

'You take the bench.'

The man's strength was unexpected, given his state. Blaine found himself unceremoniously hauled off the ground and dumped onto the still-warm seat. The man coughed so hard he nearly choked, but he seemed to recover once he'd sat down on another bench a short distance away. After that he pretty much left Blaine alone, except to spread a putrid-smelling, weather-worn blanket over him. Though the stench nearly made him sick, the warmth seeped into Blaine's body. His shivering eased.

Blaine's eyes blinked open, his mind instantly alert. A distant clank—metal striking metal—echoed like a dream through his ears. *Where had it come from?*

His hood had fallen across his face, but he could feel someone watching him. Without moving, he looked below the edge of the material and glimpsed two legs clad in a ratty pair of jeans. They moved away. And then it sounded again. *Clank.*

Shrugging off the blanket, he pushed away from the bench to investigate. He looked for the drunken man, but he was gone. In fact, the place was largely deserted.

Wonder what time it is? He glanced around for a clock, but another clank caught his attention. It was coming from the stairwell inside the station.

Walking to the entrance, he saw a man ascending the stairs to the platform, wearing a hooded jacket similar to his. Blaine couldn't see his face from behind, plus the hood was pulled low over the man's head. But it was definitely the same person who'd been staring at him.

Clank.

Blaine caught sight of a metal bar in the man's left hand as it contacted the balustrade. His heart rate quickened as he watched the slow, deliberate steps. *He's up to no good, that's for sure.*

Lighter footsteps tapped on the stairs further up. Blaine couldn't see the second person, but they sounded smaller and seemed to be in a hurry. As the man reached the landing halfway, he turned and looked up after the other person. A slow sneer spread across his mouth, the only part of his face not fully shadowed by the hood. Casually he swung the metal bar next to his leg and shifted onto the next stair, again striking a rail in the balustrade.

Recognising the threat, Blaine didn't know whether to go after him or call for help on the public payphone nearby. He glanced about. There was no sign of security anywhere. Curiosity drove him forward. The man hadn't actually done anything.

Hurrying through the disabled access gate, he climbed up the stairs. It could have been a cliff face for the effort it required. At the top, he looked up and down the platform and saw the man approaching a young woman, the only other passenger waiting.

A jumble of boisterous voices echoed up the stairwell from below. The sound of a train coming into the station added to the noise. This seemed to spur the man into action, and he rushed up to the woman and grabbed her arm.

If Blaine ever needed a hit of adrenaline, it was now. He hurried towards them, willing himself to run faster, but his legs were like cotton threads.

The young woman shrieked and tried to fend off her attacker.

She clutched her bag and hit at him repeatedly. With a start of recognition, Blaine realised she was one of Sophie's uni friends. His heart slammed against his ribcage as the man raised the metal bar high above his head.

'No. Stop! Leave her alone.'

He was only metres away when the first strike caught the young woman's shoulder. Her cry of pain gave Blaine the strength he needed to lunge forward in an attempt to put himself between her and the man's weapon.

Time seemed to go into slow motion. He hurled himself towards the woman, raising his arms to try and protect her head. As he collided with her, he felt a glancing blow on his temple, buffered slightly by the hood covering his head. Then another sickening crack sounded—metal against bone—and they toppled to the ground.

That Blaine had surprised the attacker was clear. The man's eyes betrayed drug-induced desperation. For a moment he hesitated, briefly almost lucid with the shock of his actions. The metal pipe dropped from his hand, landing with a clatter. Snatching up the women's fallen bag, he jumped off the platform, crossing the tracks in front of the incoming train. A horn blast broadcast the danger of his actions as the train came to a stop. Running along the opposite platform, the man dashed for the exit and disappeared into the dark.

Several late night travellers spilled from the carriages as shouts exploded across the platform. Blaine blocked it out, trying desperately to remember the girl's name. A slick patch of blood matted her blonde hair.

Sienna! It's the same girl Sophie met on her way home.

'Sienna, are you all right?' He was still half-lying on top of her.

'He attacked her. And another one ran across the tracks.'

'Get off her, you thug. Someone call the cops and an

ambulance, too.'

Blaine was yanked up by the shoulder, the grip that held him painful. 'I was just trying to help.' The grasp slackened and then released him. A pulsing thud had taken up residence in his temple, making him disoriented. He crawled back towards the train. A spotted trail of blood followed him.

'Hey, someone stop him.'

As the driver jumped out, Blaine realised he was precariously near the edge of the platform. He hadn't paid enough attention to his direction. Teetering, he tumbled down onto the tracks directly in front of the train. He felt a dull thud as his head hit a rail. A thunderous vibration ran through the tracks below him.

'Stop him!'

Blaine dragged himself towards the opposite platform.

'Hey, look, there's someone on the track.'

Footsteps pounded nearby and then hands reached down to help him up. 'Thank you.' His voice was slurred in his own ears. The wail of sirens echoed like shouts across a canyon.

He tried to look back—tried to see what was happening to Sophie's friend. But the train was in the way. The two men who had helped him were also looking towards the platform where Sienna had been attacked. A man yelled and pointed at Blaine from across the tracks, but his voice was drowned out by a freight train coming through the station on the city-bound line.

'What's going on?'

'Dunno.'

The freight train roared past. A long line of carriages rumbled behind the engine, their discordant groans sounding above the squeal of metal wheels against the tracks.

'Can you tell us what happened?' The man shouted above

the train.

Despite his question, Blaine lay there for a moment. The second man squeezed his shoulder.

'Hey, I'm a first aider. Do you need help? Want me to call someone?'

Blaine sat up and shook his head. 'No.' The turbulence from the train gusted about them.

'You sure? There's blood running down your face.'

'Oh.' Blaine knew he should tell the first-aider he was still a minor requiring parental consent, but he hadn't been asked and felt no compulsion to volunteer these details. Instead, he pushed back his hood and pressed his fingers to his forehead, feeling the tacky wetness. 'No, I'm okay. But can you help me up?'

An arm came around Blaine and eased him to his feet. 'Thanks.' He was relieved he could no longer see or hear the man from the other platform who had been yelling. *Why would he think I attacked Sienna?* Though he supposed it wouldn't have looked good to the people who had arrived just in time to see him knock her over.

'Why were you on the tracks?'

'I fell. Did you see what happened to that girl?'

'No. Just got here when you cracked your head on the rail. Lucky you didn't get cleaned up. You sure you don't want me to call an ambulance? That cut looks nasty.'

'No, I'm fine. Thanks.' Blaine wanted to get away before the angry man came looking for him. He knew Sienna would be cared for, but didn't need some random person shouting false accusations at him. Knowing his right to refuse first aid, he shook his head a final time and limped from the platform into the darkened alleys south of the station.

A few streets away Blaine came across a covered truck with

one of the rear doors ajar. He crawled into the back, inched his way towards the front of the flatbed and fell still, desperately in need of rest. His temple was sticky, and he realised he was still bleeding. *And I forgot my bag.*

Then his temperature began to rise.

No, not now.

But there was no stopping the fever. *Please don't let it be another seizure.* This time there would be no medical intervention.

CHAPTER 21

An armed robbery gone wrong has left a teenage university student seriously injured after she was attacked at the South Brisbane railway station late last night. The incident, which was captured on closed circuit security surveillance, saw a man approach the young woman and brazenly threaten her with a large metal bar. The teenager was resisting the assault when another man came running in, knocking her to the ground. While subduing the woman it appears the second assailant was accidentally struck in the head by the weapon of his accomplice. Police apprehended one suspect shortly after the incident, and with assistance from witnesses, have compiled a description of the other man being sought for questioning.

Sophie glanced up from her bowl of cereal, fruit and yoghurt, unable to ignore the television blaring in the background. The reporter read out a description of the suspect. She nearly choked when the police identification sketch appeared on the screen.

Blaine!

She couldn't decide if she felt more sick or sad. 'Blaine wouldn't do that.'

'Pardon, Soph?'

'Nothing, Dad.'

The security footage was replayed and Sophie froze, unable to tear her eyes away. She was sure it was Sienna being thrown to the ground by a man, while another one struck her on the head with a metal bar. The images were grainy and both men were wearing similar jackets with hoods pulled low over their faces. Was Blaine the one running at her or was he the one wielding the weapon?

> Based on evidence at the scene, police believe the second man to be injured from the altercation and are searching the area for further leads. The victim remains in hospital in a serious but stable condition.

Was Blaine hurt? Did he really attack my friend? He did say he had no money ...

All she knew was she couldn't eat another mouthful of her breakfast. Even her half-finished coffee held no appeal. Pushing back the bowl, Sophie considered ringing Sienna. Would she be well enough to talk? She didn't know Sienna's family or their contact details, except they lived in north-west New South Wales on a large property.

Sophie wondered if she should call the police and tell them Blaine's identity. But that would be directly against the instructions of the research scientists she had met yesterday. For some reason they didn't want police involvement, claiming it to be for Blaine's protection.

She had to go to South Bank as soon as she could but was hanging on a call from Blaine's mum. Sophie had rung several times the previous night, but Mrs Colton must have been hosting a perfume party or not near her phone, as it went straight to message bank. Given the circumstances, she was surprised the calls weren't taken.

Pushing back her chair, she collected her bowl and scraped the contents into the bin. Worrying her lip, she tipped the coffee down the sink drain and reflected on the conversation she'd had the previous night with Jett. He too couldn't believe what the scientists were trying to tell her about Blaine.

Yet, there is the evidence …

She glanced back towards the television. It didn't seem possible. As she'd told Blaine, *he* was one of the main reasons she'd become so interested in science. She'd gotten to know him and realised what a wonderful boy lived inside his atrophied body. She knew it would take people with determination and skill to make a difference for people like him. Besides, she always topped her mathematics and science classes, so it seemed a logical career path.

But has his gene therapy caused this streak of violence?

No. Something else must be affecting his mind, compelling such out-of-character behaviour. She just hoped she could get to him before something worse happened.

Surely Blaine will listen to me …

'Dad, I'm going to the markets at South Bank today.'

'Okay, Soph.'

He was distracted enough not to question her motive, and thankfully both her mum and Jett were working. *Then again, it would be good if Jett could come.*

Also telling her younger sister, Anna, where she was going, Sophie grabbed her mobile phone off the charger. She'd missed a call from Mrs Colton. She phoned back. 'Mrs Colton, it's Sophie. And no, I've not seen Blaine since yesterday. But did you see that television report?'

'Yes, but I find it difficult to believe. I'm sure it's the angle of the camera. What if he was trying to help?'

'It didn't look like it, and until someone can clarify otherwise ...' She weighed her next words. 'Mrs Colton, Dr Hartfield told me there's something wrong. She said he's become violent.'

'Where did you meet Melissa Hartfield? I'm not sure I trust *anything* that woman has to say.'

Sophie wondered if she would only validate Dr Hartfield's claims by explaining Blaine's strange behaviour over the past two days. Then she remembered something that might help. 'Do you know a man called Luke who might know Dr Hartfield and Blaine?'

'No. Why is that?'

Sophie tried not to let disappointment spill into her tone. She'd hoped Belinda Colton would be able to fit the pieces together. 'When I was with Dr Hartfield and Dr Jonick yesterday, a man they called Luke stopped us and started asking questions about Blaine and the gene therapy. They didn't say his last name, but he seemed to know lots about it.'

'What did Dr Hartfield say?'

'She basically shut him down. Told him it wasn't his business. He seemed pretty upset, but Dr Hartfield left him to follow me when I went after Blaine.'

'Luke?' There was a long pause. 'No, I'm sorry. It doesn't ring a bell—and certainly doesn't help us find Blaine or clear up this business at the train station. It's just so ... unlike him.'

'Look, I don't know what's going on, but Blaine asked me for a favour. He wanted me to ask if you and Mr Colton knew about his sickness before his adoption.'

Belinda Colton was silent on the other end of the phone.

'Are you still there?'

'Yes, Sophie. Why would he ask that?'

Sophie shrugged. 'Not sure. But did you know?'

'No, we didn't. We knew he had serious health issues and wasn't meeting his developmental milestones, and we knew his mother wasn't coping and was at the point of abandoning him, leaving him to his fate. But we didn't know *why* he was sick.' Her voice broke. 'We've never told him that. We didn't want him to think we hadn't wanted him.'

Sophie felt the warmth of the screen against her face. She couldn't figure out why Blaine was suddenly asking, but she could understand what it might mean to him. He hadn't been chosen, he'd been a booby prize. She wondered if that could be why he was behaving so strangely.

Belinda's strained voice sounded in her ear, snapping into her thoughts. 'Sophie, please don't mention that until Blaine's father and I can speak to him. Last night I called Mike at the conference and talked until my phone ran out of charge, but after seeing that news report I'm going to ring him again and ask him to come home immediately.'

'I understand. I don't think Mr Colton would want to be anywhere else. But can you think of any other reason why Blaine might be acting like this?'

'Not really. I was told Blaine's post-treatment assessment had been completed and he was on the way home.'

Sophie felt even more confused about the claims of Blaine

exhibiting violent behaviour. From what Mrs Colton had said, he'd lied about not being able to go home. 'Blaine seemed to think they were waiting for him to go home so they could capture him. It sounds ridiculous, but have you noticed anyone unusual hanging around the house?'

'Well, I've not even considered that. I can look out front now, but I've not noticed anything. I also don't understand why Dr Hartfield would be trying to hold him against his will … unless she wanted to speak to him?'

Sophie waited while Belinda studied the street outside her house, providing a brief description as she did. 'Nothing unusual?'

'No,' Belinda confirmed. 'We need to find Blaine and work out what's going on. If he's as unwell as they claim, then it's not likely he'll be travelling far. I still don't believe he would attack anyone. How could he if he were so weak?'

Sophie chewed her lip some more. 'Good point. I was about to go to South Bank to meet him. He asked if I could get some medication from you and bring it to him. What's that about?' She heard a sigh on the other end of the line.

'Unfortunately, with Blaine now out of the institute's care, he's not receiving the medication he needs to function. His decline will be rapid if he doesn't take some soon.'

Her heart stalled. 'You mean … You mean he could die?'

'Either that or be rendered incapacitated by high fever, seizures or even stroke, which he risks if he stops taking the medication for even a week.'

Feeling like she couldn't breathe, Sophie realised how tightly she was holding the phone to her ear. *She* had *to meet Blaine—as soon as possible.*

If only Jett were here.

'Mrs Colton, I'm heading to South Bank now. I'll come by your house and get some of the medication. Based on what you've said, he may not have much time.'

'I should stay here in case Blaine comes home.'

'But he promised to meet me.'

'And he keeps his promises.' Belinda paused, evidently weighing her options. 'I'll meet you there and bring some Ramer's Cure. Maybe I can even convince Blaine to come home with me.'

'That'd be great. I'll see you soon.'

Sophie hung up the phone and closed her eyes to stem the tears that were threatening.

'Sophie?'

She looked up. Her father was standing beside her. She wondered how long he'd been listening. 'Blaine could die, Dad.' A sob caught in her throat and she turned into his arms.

'Oh, sweetheart.' He held her close and gently patted her back. 'Anna and I are coming—no argument. Now let's go find him.'

CHAPTER 22

Blaine blinked awake and squinted at the shaft of light that split the darkness. The truck's door rattled as it was unlatched. He lay perfectly still, hoping not to be noticed.

Sometime during the night he'd had a vague awareness of being driven somewhere. He had no idea where he was or what he should do next. In fact, he was beginning to wonder if it was worth hiding at all. Melissa Hartfield would track him down eventually, and then what? He couldn't exactly go to the authorities—he was illegal.

Mostly, he was so hungry his stomach seemed to be eating itself.

Two men began loading goods into the truck. Blaine crept closer to the front and wedged himself between a great pile of canvas and a stack of metal pipes.

'First we'll deliver those tents to St. Lucia for that careers event at the Uni of Queensland next week, then we'll do our drop-offs on the way to Mowbray Park.'

'It's the medium marquee we're setting up, right?'

'Yeah. The wedding is at ten in the morning. Decorators and caterers are keen to get in ASAP.'

Soon they'd finished loading. The door closed with a resounding bang.

Mowbray Park? I'm heading back to nearly where I started—eventually ...

Blaine sat up straight. *Sophie! What time is it?*

As the men walked around to the front of the vehicle, he heard them talking about the South Bank attack the previous evening. 'All over the news,' one of them said. As Blaine listened, he was disturbed to realise the police were looking for him.

Do they really think I attacked Sienna? Wouldn't it have been obvious I was trying to help?

He realised too, that if it was 'all over the news', his mum along with Sophie and her family would have probably seen the incident.

What must they think?

The truck took off at a good pace and Blaine was jostled into the canvas. His head still hurt, but all things considered, he felt pretty good after a decent night's sleep. Then again, he hadn't had to exert himself either.

As he lay in the darkness, his mind explored the flashbacks he'd had last night. Dreams weren't quite the word. These kind of memories were usually associated with his seizures, though he was pretty sure he hadn't convulsed.

For some reason he couldn't get past the signing of the forms attached to his gene therapy. His parents' dilemma—their belief that he wouldn't understand the process—pooled deep in his mind. Little had they known how aware he was. Their concerns had seemed centred on their inability to justify his potential suffering, or even death, if the therapy went wrong, but he began to wonder if there was more to those eavesdropped conversations than he had previously thought.

Had they intentionally signed away his right to live beyond the shadow of ARI? If what Melissa Hartfield said was true, they had essentially sold him for nothing, with no guarantee of any returns. Was he just an inconvenience; better living out his days as an object of study?

Do they regret adopting me, after all?

Deep within, he knew Dr Hartfield wasn't lying about the timing of his diagnosis. And this revelation had plagued him ever since.

He'd never doubted his parents' love for him until the past week. They'd always reminded him time and again of how priceless he was to them. They claimed they'd been handpicked by divine intervention to rescue him and offer him a safe and loving home in which to live. Or so they had said ...

But I was never supposed to live beyond ten years of age ...

Could their constant insistence that he was God's chosen son for them be merely a cover to hide the shock of his diagnosis and the great inconvenience of his continued existence? Had he outlived his usefulness?

Perhaps his parents were weary of his care. It seemed they were willing to try anything that promised therapeutic benefits. In fact, the Ramer trials weren't his first brush with gene therapy.

The truck took a sharp corner and Blaine rolled hard against the tough tarpaulin body cover. He shifted to make himself more comfortable, taking care to avoid the metal supports of the framework. Without seeing the road, he was beginning to feel queasy. Adding to this, uncertainty sat like a block of ice in his stomach. He felt cold from the inside out.

Surely my parents did not elect for me to be subjected to the trials because they'd had enough of caring for me? Would they protect me from Dr Hartfield if she told them of my illegal status?

The seed of doubt began to grow roots that wound through his heart, creating fissures in all the certainties of his life.

Blaine tried to remain patient as the men went about their drop-offs. Some locations seemed to take forever, which he figured meant they also had to set-up what they were delivering. Other stops just involved a quick offload.

Each time they retrieved gear, Blaine held his breath as he hid. One man had even stood right next to the canvas he was lying under. Sweat had popped out on his brow as he'd tried to keep perfectly still.

Not wanting to get caught out, Blaine resisted the temptation to leave the truck when they stopped. This ride was going where he needed. Even if he arrived later than he'd planned, his few remaining silver coins weren't going to take him there any faster.

Knowing he'd have to walk the distance from the park to South Bank, Blaine decided to take the second half of Ramer's Cure. It was much easier to see while the rear door was open, letting in light. He hoped the medication would be enough to stabilise him for the rest of the day.

Blaine frowned at the bag as he swallowed and noticed a tiny shard wedged in the corner. *That's right, the third piece. It's not much, but it's better than nothing.*

He put the small bag back into his pocket and zipped it closed. Soon he'd have all the Cure he needed. Blaine just hoped Sophie would wait.

Blaine could only guess the time when the men started talking wedding marquees.

'Let's get moving. Call Nick and Rob. If they're finished at the other sites, they can come over and give us a hand.'

'Sure. Might even have time for a decent lunch.'

They laughed, but Blaine silently groaned. *Lunch? He* didn't have time for lunch. *As soon as that door opens, I'm outta here.*

CHAPTER 23

The truck wheezed and squeaked to a stop. Blaine scrambled to the rear door and waited. He crouched beside tall stacks of plastic chairs, figuring he'd have the advantage of surprise if they saw him.

His pulse whoomphed in his ears, his muscles strained with expectancy. But the door didn't move. He blew out a sigh. *Seriously? They've gone for lunch?*

He couldn't tell for sure if they had just stopped or the men were off having a picnic somewhere. After waiting for a while, he decided to take matters into his own hands and started fishing around to see how the tarpaulin side curtains were secured. Squatted down, concentrating on his task, he heard the clatter of the door latch too late.

'Oy! What are you doing?'

Blaine spun on his heels and shaded his eyes against the burst of sunlight. He heard the man jump into the back and come towards him. Squinting to see better, he dodged across the width of the truck, knowing the man's sidekick wouldn't be far behind.

'Frank, we've got a stowaway.'

'Dude, I just needed a ride. I didn't touch anything.' Blaine inched around him, trying to get nearer the door. The man's doughy waistline betrayed a fondness for meal breaks. *Bet I'm faster than him ...*

'Fraaaaank!'

Blaine sprung towards the door. He'd been right. Even when his footing slipped on some tent poles, dough-man didn't stand a chance. But as he leaped for the exit, Frank appeared, partly-eaten burger in hand and lettuce hanging out his mouth.

'Hey, it's that kid the cops are after.' Half-chewed food tumbled down the front of Frank's shirt as he tried to block the way.

Blaine hesitated for a millisecond. The clang of metal poles striking together announced dough-man's movement and jarred him alert. Heart pounding, he ran forward and jumped as high as he could, hoping to hurdle over Frank.

Still grasping the burger, Frank caught his ankle and knocked him to the ground. Kicking and writhing, Blaine managed to disengage the hand on his foot. He rolled to his feet as he pushed Frank back, sending the burger flying, and then ran as fast as he could with no thought of direction. His only goal was escape.

By the time he reached Lytton Road, Blaine was relieved he'd taken the second fragment of Ramer's Cure earlier. A public phone across the street caught his eye, but Frank still tailed him at a distance. Crossing the road, he jogged down a side street, hoping the man would soon give up.

Chest near to bursting, he had to stop. His heart sank when he realised the sun was high overhead. It had to be past midday. *Has Sophie waited? If only I had my phone.*

Blaine settled into an easy pace as he walked across Kangaroo Point. He determined to keep an eye out for another public payphone and call Sophie when he was certain the agitated tent guys were no longer pursuing him. Despite his leisurely stride, he may as well been sprinting for the effort it took. At least he'd had enough reserves to get away from Frank and friend.

It didn't take long for Blaine's confidence in his physical abilities to erode. Having had so little medication over the past two weeks, he knew his condition was unpredictable. Just when it seemed he could walk for hours, strangling fatigue overran him.

Sitting down on the roadside gutter, he allowed the warm winter sun to melt through him. Its power re-energised him like a photovoltaic cell. He closed his eyes as cars zinged past just metres away.

Soon he was back on his feet. He looked up and down the road, trying to decide the best direction to take. From his memories of 'you are here' maps, none of the streets offered a direct route across. He decided to continue south and work his way in the direction of South Bank via streets running east-west.

What would have seemed a simple task two weeks ago, now left him in a cold sweat and unsteady on his legs. When Blaine reached a recreation park, he figured he wasn't even halfway across the Point. *Not gonna break any land-speed records today.*

When he finally trudged up Walmsley Street, he felt like he was trying to breathe inside a sealed plastic bag. And he'd completely forgotten to look for phone booths. Every bit of strength had been consumed with staying stable on his feet.

With a tortoise-rivelling pace, he eventually crossed over River Terrace. A glance at the sun, now leaning towards the west, told Blaine what he didn't want to know. It had taken ages, even though he was barely a kilometre from his start point.

Using the opportunity to rest on the narrow strip of parkland, he leaned on his elbows against the barrier. The Botanic Gardens were directly across the water, with the cityscape nestled in behind. Beyond the railing, the Kangaroo Point Cliffs plunged down to the river. *Well, at least it's not uphill.* It felt like he'd scaled inclines most of the way.

Blaine bent to finger the cargo pocket of his jeans. He was comforted by the slight irregularity of the small clip-seal bag that contained the splinter of Ramer's Cure. Yet, even once he had free access to his meds, it didn't change the reality of Melissa Hartfield's claim.

He'd never heard of anyone being an illegal GMO. *One of the perks of receiving groundbreaking gene therapy.* He scoffed. The idea of living out his life in that observation room made his head float.

Resolve settled within him as he studied the afternoon scene. As his eyes followed the progress of a CityCat on a diagonal course across the river, his goal became clear.

He had to find Professor Ramer.

But how?

CHAPTER 24

'It's getting late, Sophie. We need to go—and unless you've called in, you need to get to work.'

Sophie nodded but otherwise didn't respond to her father's prompt. He knew how much she needed the money from her part-time job to make the repayments on the shiny new Mazda 3 she and Jett co-owned. He also expected her to honour her commitments, including the one to her employer and workmates. Yet, for Blaine, she'd be willing to risk disappointing her boss and beg a loan from her parents for the month.

Anna hung off their father's hand. She was exhausted from the hours spent searching for Blaine. Even the upbeat markets did nothing to entice her.

They had waited for Blaine for an hour, before her dad suggested they search the surrounding regions. They had covered every square metre of South Bank, extended their search, and then worked their way back. There was no sign of him.

At South Brisbane train station, Sophie couldn't help but notice dark red stains marking the platform beyond the yellow safety zone, right at the edge of the platform. It looked like blood.

Was it missed in the clean up from the previous night? Could it be Blaine's?

The image from the television appeared in her mind. In the facial identification sketch, they had drawn the suspect in a way that made him look serious, even menacing. Not like Blaine at all. Something was very wrong with the whole situation and she wished she could ask more questions of Dr Hartfield and Dr Jonick.

She had been startled by Dr Jonick's vigorous effort to reach Blaine. It was only by millimetres Blaine had escaped. Even stranger, when she introduced herself to Melissa Hartfield, it was as if the doctor already knew who she was. Sophie was certain they'd never met.

Perhaps Blaine mentioned me?

She could only wish.

Quickening her steps to catch up with her father and sister, she noticed her dad was again on the phone to Belinda Colton. Blaine's mother had gone home just after midday, in case he'd changed his mind and headed there. Even though she was optimistic of her son's return, Sophie was certain he wasn't going to turn up home anytime soon.

Her chest squeezed painfully as they walked past the Maritime Museum, back along Riverwalk towards the car park. The familiar settings they passed held so many wonderful memories.

Without warning, images of last New Year's Day jumped into her mind. It was so vivid she could nearly feel Blaine's nearness as he'd bent his head near to hers, their eyes locked, his lips just centimetres from her own—only to have Jett shatter the moment with his announcement of ice cream. *What if Jett hadn't brought ice cream for us all?*

She shivered and knew without doubt she couldn't turn Blaine into the police without speaking to him first. But perhaps it was best if the researchers knew ...

'You okay, Sophie?'

Sophie's head came around and she forced her mouth into a weary smile. 'Yes, I just miss him and wish we could find him.'

'Me too, Soph.'

'Ice cream!'

Anna had, moments before, been dragging behind her father. Now she was jumping up and down, pointing at an ice cream cart. Sophie laughed. 'You are *so* like Jett.'

Their father chuckled, but swiftly grew sombre. Sophie realised he was still on the phone to Mrs Colton.

She reached into her bag and wrapped her fingers about her mobile phone. 'Dad, can you ask if Mrs Colton thinks I should call Dr Hartfield?'

Sophie's father transferred the message. He nodded, looking as if the small action took his last drop of energy. Sophie could only imagine what Blaine's mother might be saying—and feeling. 'Yeah, Sophie, guess you should. Talk soon, Belinda.'

The lines around her father's eyes deepened as he ended the call.

'How's Mrs Colton?'

'Not good.' He sighed and slipped the phone into his pocket. 'She said Mike's catching the first flight home he can. She doesn't trust Dr Hartfield but she keeps on saying how she feels this could be their fault; that maybe they shouldn't have sent him for the treatment; that maybe he was better off ...'

His words hung unfinished, but Sophie knew what he was trying to say. Blaine's life was at risk; he seemed to have lost all reasoning and was exhibiting irrational behaviour. All because of the treatment intended to save his life.

'Perhaps it's a misunderstanding. Blaine *seemed* fine when I was with him yesterday.'

Her father offered a weak smile. 'Call them, Sophie. Better sooner than later.'

How does one find a man who doesn't seem to exist anymore? Granted, that wasn't entirely true. However, based on the remarks Blaine had overheard during his containment at ARI, it seemed Professor Ramer had finally obtained the breakthrough he was seeking and then disappeared. *How did that happen—and why?*

A structure caught his eye in a northward direction—*uphill.* With a groan, he noticed something in the distance, on the opposite side of the road. *Phone booth.*

I can call Sophie, and if I'm lucky it'll have a phone book. He hoped that if Professor Ramer still lived in Brisbane, his number would be listed. *Otherwise I could try to find that Luke guy who worked with the Professor.* He wished he'd thought of asking when he ran into the man.

For now, the public payphone was his best option.

CHAPTER 25

Sophie dialled Dr Hartfield's mobile number and waited for the call to connect. Even as the ring tone droned in her ear, she secretly hoped there would be no answer. But it only took a few seconds for Dr Hartfield to pick up.

Conscious that her phone was nearly flat, she kept the conversation brief as she spoke of seeing Blaine the previous evening, before providing details of the news report of the train station incident. Even as she mentioned their futile search for him that day, Dr Hartfield kept pushing the 'Blaine could be dangerous' point, as if not finding him may have saved them from some unspoken harm. Sophie wanted to yell at the woman, whose voice was tinny with insincerity and fact-finding calculation, reminding her that *she'd* known Blaine most of her life and whatever impression Dr Hartfield had from the blip in time she'd been associated with him meant *nothing* compared to the voice inside her saying Blaine was innocent. Instead, she meekly repeated that he hadn't tried to harm her.

Tears smudged her vision as she ended the call. She felt like a traitor. *Blaine, surely you're around here somewhere.*

Making one final glance up and down the river, she crossed over to the stairwell leading to the underground car park. Somehow the stairs represented their defeat. She racked her mind as to what else she could do to help her friend.

Sienna.

'Dad, can you and Anna go on ahead and pay our parking fee? I won't be a minute.'

Sophie unlocked her screen, dialled Sienna's number and waited. Her battery charge indicator had been red for a while now. She hoped the phone wouldn't die before she could ask what she needed to. If Sienna was out of hospital, surely she'd have her mobile on. The call went straight to message bank. Sophie left a voicemail and asked her friend to call when she got a chance.

Only after she'd hung up, did she realise the phone had probably been stolen along with Sienna's bag. She'd have to figure out another way to make contact.

With a sadness that numbed her chest like anaesthetic, Sophie trudged down the stairs to her waiting father and sister. They walked silently to the car.

Dad took the driver's seat, despite it being her and Jett's car. With everything going on, she felt too distracted to drive, especially being a recent provisional 'P-plate' licence holder.

When they had left the car park, Dad flicked on the radio to listen to the news. She felt even worse when she realised who was making headlines.

Police have received numerous calls in response to a brutal robbery at South Brisbane train station last night. Several sightings of the man who escaped the scene have since been reported, including two workers who alleged they were assaulted by the suspect at Mowbray Park earlier today. Authorities have issued a request for information on a young Mitochondrial Disease survivor linked to Advance Research Institute, in relation to these attacks. The young man's parents, who reside locally, have declined to comment on their son's possible involvement in these incidents.

Anyone who comes in contact with the suspect is asked not to approach this potentially dangerous young man. Police have requested that anyone with information regarding his location contact them immediately on—

Sophie pushed the 'off' button and silenced the radio. The constant humming of the car engine replaced the offending voice of the reporter. 'At least we know where he's been.' Her voice was flat. Mowbray Park wasn't that far away. He'd stood her up.

She tried not to sniff and give herself away, but knew she wasn't fooling anyone when her dad reached across and squeezed her shoulder. Sophie opened the glove box and pulled out a tissue pack. Wiping her eyes then blowing her nose, she silently prayed Blaine would be kept safe and that somehow this mess would soon be sorted.

Blaine trudged up the path towards the familiar, bold colours advertising the payphone's location. He had memorised Sophie's mobile number and knew she'd have it on. Sophie worked in a restaurant on weekends but, given she'd offered to meet him, Blaine assumed she wasn't rostered on today.

When he reached the phone, he fed in some coins, dialled the number and cradled the receiver against his ear. The sound of his heartbeat throbbing in his ears nearly drowned out the ringtone.

'Hello?'

His heart gave a small jump. 'Sophie, it's Blaine.'

'Blaine! Where are you?' Her tone was sharper than he expected.

'I'm sorry. I got held up.' It was too hard to explain all that had happened. 'Where are you?'

'We're nearly home from South Bank after spending most of the day searching for *you*. Why didn't you call earlier, *before* they started saying things about you on the media?'

'Like what?'

'Like, instead of meeting me, you attacked two men at Mowbray Park.'

'That's rubbish. Did they *say* it was me?'

'No, but it wasn't hard to join the dots. *Were* you at Mowbray Park today?'

'Yes, but *they* were trying to get *me*.'

'And then stuff about you hurting Sienna at South Brisbane station and getting hurt yourself. There was video footage. Was that really you?'

'It was me, but that's not the way it happened, Soph—'

'Were you hurt like they said?'

'I'm okay. Well, I'm not really. I've only got a few cents left and I need that medication—fast.' Blaine watched the phone's digital display and pressed the received harder against his head, as if that would bring Sophie closer. The call wouldn't last long.

'I have it with me—though I'm supposed to be at work soon. Are you at South Bank?'

'No. I'm not at South Bank, I'm—'

The phone cut out before he could finish. 'No! Stupid phone.' He was sure he hadn't run out of credit yet. *What happened?* Digging about in his pocket, he fed in the last of the coins. It was just enough, and would hopefully enable him to finish what he had to say. The phone rang but went directly to message bank. *Awesome. Why would she turn her phone off?*

Determined not to waste the last of his funds, he waited for Sophie's 'Sorry I missed your call: you've got ten seconds to leave a message … go!' to run through. Anticipating the prompt tone, words strained ready at his mouth, like sprinters awaiting the starter's gun. *Wish there was a button to skip straight to speaking.* A surge of adrenaline made his hands shake when the signal sounded. 'Sophie, I *really* need Ramer's Cure. Fast. I'm not at South Bank right now, but could you or Mum meet me at the—'

A beep marked the end of his message time and he clattered the receiver against the cradle with extra force, even before the 'your message will be sent as a text' spiel had begun. He felt like the key to a secret treasure chest had dropped through his clumsy fingers. *Stupid mitochondrial disease. Stupid therapy.*

Now he had no money at all and his stomach was roaring at him.

And there's no phone book, either. He rummaged about his mind to try and remember the directory assistance number. A memory sparked. *1223*—that's it. Quickly he dialled and responded to the pre-recorded voice prompts.

'No listing for Ramer. Of course.' He plonked down the receiver and turned away, slapping the side of the booth with his palm as he left. A group of passersby stopped to stare. Realising

152

the attention he'd drawn, Blaine kept moving.

He glanced across the river at QUT, figuring it was unlikely there would be free campus activities on the weekend. There was a TAFE college a short distance away and Griffith Uni also had a campus nearby, but Blaine had no idea of their weekend social activities either. Besides, he couldn't scavenge forever.

He had to get some cash.

CHAPTER 26

Blaine continued in the direction of South Bank Parklands. He hoped beyond hope Sophie would come back, now he had contacted her. Along the way, he tried asking pedestrians if they could spare some change. He didn't even get past the word 'spare' before most people made a wide berth about him, all but jogging in the other direction.

His body was hot but Blaine still shivered as he followed the quieter side streets downhill. Eventually he emerged at the river. Clouds had begun to cluster overhead, shadowing the sun. *Great. Rain would make this day just perfect.* Distracted by a more pressing need, he was relieved to spot some public toilets a short distance away, in a more secluded area along the river.

Quivering from head to toe, he made it to the facilities. He had finished washed his hands when an overpowering weakness dragged him to his knees. Face against the sink, he let the coolness of the metal bring relief to his burning forehead.

The tiled floor was cold against his knees. Blaine let himself slide, fully prone, below the hand basin. Even though he was hot, he shivered violently.

It was then he noticed a discarded five dollar pre-paid phonecard on the floor behind the plumbing. It was caught in a spider's web.

A pre-paid calling card? Reaching out, he picked up the card and held it before his eyes. *Does it have any credit on it? Could I be so lucky?*

It's not luck, Blaine.

His mother's words echoed in his mind as if she stood right next to him. He wondered if he'd ever hear her voice for real again.

Do you think any of this has been luck, darling?

He remembered how patient his parents had been with him. For so many years they had nursed and fed, bathed and changed, loved and sung, played and given.

And yet I doubt them so easily? Hope gained another small tick.

Blaine pressed the calling card into his pocket, web and all. Pushing his chest away from the floor, he failed to reach a sitting position and was too tired to make it outside. Although he'd determined he could survive on a half dose every second day, Blaine knew he needed Ramer's Cure now. All he had was a miniscule fragment.

Fumbling out the bag, he managed to undo the clip-seal and get the last crumb into his mouth. His hands shook as he pushed the bag back into the zippered pocket on the leg of his jeans.

The medication needed to build up in his system to work, so he doubted such a tiny dose would have any effect. Even so, he hoped for some relief from the dreadful exhaustion pinning him on the tiles.

It never came. He crawled into the large disabled access cubicle. Trembling all the way into the corner furthermost from the toilet, he crumpled in a heap.

'Hi, Eddie, looking good.'

'You too, Mel.'

Eddie wished Melissa had worn something a little less provocative. Her white, backless, halter-neck dress with a plunging neckline made it difficult to remember she was only using him. It reminded him of the classic Marilyn Monroe dress, only with less material. Although she had a jacket slung over her arm, he was sure she must have been cold.

Her perfume lingered between them. Eddie tried not to think about how good she smelled. The citrusy sweetness was fresh and light—his favourite of her fragrance collection. He couldn't help thinking how much this contrasted the undertones he'd discovered in her nature.

He was unsure what he hoped to achieve meeting her under the guise of a date, but when the timing was right, he intended to push for an explanation on her deception. Knowing her, that could cost him his career. He dug his hands into the pockets of his new designer jeans and motioned the way forward with his head. 'Where to?'

Melissa sighed. 'I don't know, Eddie. Why don't you choose?'

Her manner was abnormally blithe for his liking. Casual and carefree were two words *never* associated with Melissa Hartfield—unless she had an ulterior motive. *What are you cooking up in that head of yours, Mel?*

They wandered towards Riverwalk. He measured his stride to Melissa's unhurried pace. 'I often come in for a run on the weekends. It's a great way to see the city.'

'True.' Melissa nodded. 'Though I think the city always looks prettier at night.'

'Good ol' QUT.' Eddie took a moment to survey the familiar structures on the other side of the river. He'd done his undergrad and honours through that institute, before moving to Melbourne for his doctorate. It had been a grand adventure leaving home and meeting new people. He'd also developed great enthusiasm for research in the field of human congenital disease, specialising in genetic disorders.

He smiled as he remembered the fun times. On moving to Victoria, he'd relished the independence, dived into the gym scene and participated in uni games for track and field. And there he'd met Alyce.

Like someone drawing in cold air, he sucked back these thoughts and tucked them away in a safe, secluded part of his mind. No, he wasn't going to think about her anymore. He'd decided that recently. Instead, he let his thoughts settle on his years with ARI.

He glanced at Melissa, who seemed oblivious to his distance. She was an attractive woman—on the surface.

How different things had been when Professor Ramer was the institute's Director. Although Eddie had never been in Ramer's research group, the advances of ARI as a whole had been groundbreaking. Ramer seemed to inject enthusiasm into every person working within the organisation. For a time, Eddie had been caught up in the excitement long enough to stop thinking about Alyce. But soon the pain returned, so he'd portrayed himself as an uncaring jerk.

Good one, Eddie.

Ramer had expected hard work out of his associates, but he was also fair. That same ethos translated across the diverse research entities operating out of the institute. Eddie had relished the opportunity to be researching in his discipline of choice, within such a well-funded, respected organisation. He'd also learned a lot from Professor Ramer through the twice-weekly lunchtime lectures that provided each group an opportunity to present their research to their colleagues, thus expanding his knowledge of genetic disorders and challenging his own investigative approaches.

And then Melissa had joined the company ...

A cyclist sped past them and Eddie instinctively side-stepped, bumping into Melissa as he did. 'Sorry.' She shrugged away his concern and Eddie again wondered where her thoughts were at.

With all the competitiveness she exuded in the workplace, it was hard to imagine a different side to her. Unfortunately that drive had only translated into small advances in her research. He suspected it would only be a matter of time before a 'please explain' would be demanded by the funding bodies.

I might not have brought in the same money as her, but I always met my projected outcomes. She can never throw that in my face.

'I've had enough walking. Let's browse the markets.'

'Fine.' Eddie followed Melissa away from Riverwalk, through South Bank Parklands.

He swiftly wearied of the markets, but she didn't seem to notice. She also started leaning into him at every possible opportunity. When she linked her arm with his, Eddie decided it was time for a pre-emptive strike.

'Say, Mel, I've been wondering where the research notes for Ramer's group ended up? Surely he had to secure them somewhere if, as you claim, he's "dropped off the planet" and is no longer in communication with the PI or his group.'

That did it. Immediately she dropped her arm and swung around to face him.

'With the funding body. Why?'

Come on, Mel, you can do better than that. 'Tell me again how you determined there had been a breach of ethics? Did you read the protocol? Revise the study materials?'

'You know I can't.'

Eddie tilted his head and frowned. 'Then on what grounds are your safety concerns founded? Did ethics raise an issue? The PI? The clinical trials unit head?' *Remember, I'm just an inconsequential staff scientist. What would I know?*

Melissa laughed with a tone that hinted of bitterness. 'I noticed some inconsistencies in the summary reports I sign off on … made me curious enough to probe further. All *you* need to know is there was an issue. It's a commercial-in-confidence thing.'

She moved away to examine some natural skincare products. As he waited, Eddie let these statements turn over in his mind. Did she *really* think he was swallowing her explanations anymore? *Why did I* ever *believe her?* More questions formed that he knew she couldn't answer, and he put them to his colleague the moment she returned. 'How come you receive those reports again? And how did you make that safety determination when you don't have the investigator's documents?'

Melissa's sigh was audible. She reached up to rub her neck. Eddie wondered if she was trying to distract him as she lifted lengths of her straight, blonde hair and exposed her bare back.

'I submitted a written request, but I pretty much know what Ramer did anyway.'

'At least you *think* you do …'

She dropped her arms, letting her hair tumble over her shoulders. Eddie felt the stab of her gaze. 'Don't get too presumptuous, Dr Jonick. I'm still Principal Scientist on your current research grants.'

She winked as if teasing. But he knew she wasn't.

Threats, lovely lady? I struck a nerve there. It was time to tangle the web. 'Look, I know it's separate to our work, but surely Blaine's advances warrant further investigation. Don't you think *someone* should pick that up, given it seems Ramer's not going to?'

Her eyes brightened greedily. 'Exactly.'

'What I don't get is why you only receive a summary report? Is anyone doing deeper analysis on the data and advancing the project to the next stage? I thought the license stayed with the facility. So why's Ramer still co-coordinator? Didn't he forfeit that right when he left?' *I'm nearly as good at this bamboozling as you are, m'lady.*

He watched her fingers tense about her handbag strap. 'For whatever reason, Ramer went to a lot of trouble to set some unprecedented restrictions on my knowledge of the project and his forwarding address. Both the committee and funding bodies evidently agreed.'

This was the first statement she'd made all afternoon that Eddie felt he could *mostly* trust.

'All I know, Eddie, is I have a responsibility to ensure everyone meets their expectations. If I think there's an issue, I *will* take action to bring it to account. As for future advances, if I can expose Ramer's incompetence and negligence, whilst gaining a more intimate understanding of his therapeutic approaches, I figure that might just give me a leg up when the funding body starts looking for a new research head to advance their work. Maybe those resources might even fall to *our* investigative team.'

A hint of a thought crept into Eddie's mind as he mulled on her words. There were so many pieces that only half fit together, like a wooden puzzle that had been poorly jig-sawed. For one, why was she attempting to hold Blaine, when it was clear there was no safety or ethics breach? Secondly, if this rush-to-the head idea was to identify the mechanisms of Ramer's therapy whilst discrediting him, *why* was she so desperate for extra funding when she'd landed several significant grants in recent years?

Dots started connecting and Eddie knew pressure was being

exerted from somewhere. Melissa had always exhibited an obsessive drive to outdo Ramer in any way she could, but this was bigger than that. It had to be connected to money. *Dirty money?*

An alarm sounded within him, like a distant siren. Clearly there was more to this than he had ever imagined.

CHAPTER 27

Sleep had claimed Blaine so soundly he could scarcely rouse. Someone was shaking his shoulder. He tried opening his eyes, but they felt glued shut.

'Should we take him to the hospital? It's not far.'

'Or call the police. He's probably on drugs.'

'Just call the ambulance.'

The shaking stopped. Blaine turned his head and forced his heavy eyelids open a sliver. He glimpsed a man in exercise gear leaving the cubicle while talking to someone on a mobile phone. Another man was standing at the door, arms folded, watching him. He jumped forward, calling for his friend.

'He's waking up.'

The man who'd been shaking Blaine reappeared, phone still to his ear. 'He's starting to respond. Yeah, a young male, I'd say late teens. Has got a head injury. Fair bit of blood down his face and clothes, but the blood's dry and the wound doesn't seem to be bleeding anymore.' He angled the phone away from his mouth. 'The ambos are on their way.'

Groaning, Blaine struggled into a sitting position. 'I don't need an ambulance. I'm okay.' The stiffness of his body from sleeping on the cement floor made it hard to move.

'Do you know your name? Do you know where you are?'

'*Yes.*' Easing to his feet, Blaine's stomach growled a protest that matched his pointed tone.

'He's saying he's okay and is up and walking. Doesn't seem disoriented.'

'I slept in a loo. Lame, huh? I *don't* need an ambulance. But I do need to call my mum.'

The man smiled. 'They're on their way? Thanks.' He pulled the phone back again and asked more questions. 'What's your name?'

Blaine clamped his mouth shut and shook his head.

'Date of birth? Residential address?'

Still he refused to respond.

'He won't say, sorry. What about any pre-existing medical conditions?'

I don't think so. He folded his arms with as much attitude as he could muster. 'I said, I *don't* need an ambulance.'

'Look, he's not cooperating. That's all I can tell you, sorry. Okay. Yeah, at the public toilets. Thanks.' The man ended the call and slid the phone into the armband hugging his biceps.

'Here, we'll help you get cleaned up while we wait. You can use my exercise towel, but it's a bit sweaty.'

'Thanks.'

Blaine went to the basin, shrugged off his jacket and placed it on the benchtop beside the sink. Glancing back, he knew he'd never dare tell his parents he'd slept in a toilet cubicle. His father's hygiene expectations would be shattered. No doubt they'd want to bathe him in disinfectant and burn his clothes.

Despite the chill in the air, he inflicted a cold bird bath upon himself, eagerly receiving the donated towel from his self-appointed guardians. Scrubbing at a stain on his tee-shirt, Blaine noticed the men studying the bruising along his arms from the injections, drips and blood tests he'd had while at ARI.

Quickly he put down the towel and pulled his jacket back on, but he could sense them tempering their responses.

'You do drugs?' The man who had called the paramedics followed the lead of his fitness buddy and retreated back towards the entrance.

''Course not.' But Blaine knew he certainly *looked* the part of a drug user. 'Just had some tests done.'

'Right. Ambulance won't be long.'

'I'm *not* an addict.' He trailed them outside, realising it was now quite dark.

'Hey, if you're right waiting with the patient, I'm going to finish up on the stairs. I'll be back soon. That was a killer boot camp session.'

'Sure. We should be fine until the ambos come. I'll catch up after that, if you're not done beforehand.'

'Okay. Good luck, kid.' The second man ran off along the path, towards the cliffs. The rock face was strategically lit for nighttime abseiling groups.

Blaine walked over to a bench facing the water. The man followed and sat beside him. Along the river parkland were groups of people with hands on hips or knees, bent over with sweat-dampened hair and clothes. Some were stretching in the bright patches beaming from light poles. Others seemed to have worked so hard they couldn't quite decide what to do next.

Boot camp. Blaine smiled.

'My friend, Jett, is a dedicated gym goer and tried talking me into doing some boot camp sessions with him before Christmas last year.' He pitched his head towards the group. 'Looks fun, if you're into self-imposed torture.'

The man chuckled. 'Yeah, it's hard work. But gets great results.'

Blaine continued to observe. Jett was always seeking the next physical challenge. His robust, athletic build contrasted notably with Blaine's comparatively finer physique.

He was not ignorant of the effect Jett had when he walked past a group of teenage girls. It reminded Blaine of a band of puppies bounding after a throw toy. Jett tended to sport an awkward grin and flush slightly, pretending he couldn't hear the statements of admiration tumbling after him. Sophie would just roll her eyes.

'Here's the ambulance.' The man stood up, turned and waved to catch their attention. Blaine followed his lead.

There were no sirens or flashing lights. Clearly it wasn't being viewed as a high-level emergency. Blaine's nerves prickled as the paramedics walked across the shadowed car park towards him.

'Hi mate, I'm Gary. Want to come over to the ambulance so we can take a better look at you?'

Blaine crossed his arms and scowled at the pair, a man and a woman, hoping to intimidate them. 'Really, I'm *fine*.'

'Well, we're here now, so why don't you come on over and we can do a quick check? Won't take long.' The male paramedic had an upbeat manner that immediately put Blaine at ease. Resigned, he followed them and plonked himself down as directed at the back of the van. 'And sir …' He looked to the man waiting with Blaine. '… do you mind having a chat to my colleague so we can get some contact details and other info? We can take it from there.'

'Sure. But he wouldn't even give me his name.'

The Good Samaritan talked to the other medical attendant while Blaine was assessed.

'Seems you've given yourself a pretty good knock to the head.'

Gary let out a short whistle as he inspected the wound. 'How'd that happen?'

'Got hit. Fell.'

'With what? A crowbar?'

Closer than you realise, dude ...

'Any other injuries I should know about?'

'No.'

'What about nausea? Blurred vision?'

Blaine shook his head as Gary produced some equipment and clipped a sensor on Blaine's finger. 'What's your name, mate?'

Maybe first name wouldn't hurt. 'Blaine.'

'Oh good, you remember now.' He winked, making his patient smile. 'Last name?' When Blaine only shrugged, the paramedic sighed. 'Thought that might be the case. You secret agents always keep to a first name basis.'

Blaine squelched a laugh at the corny comeback.

'I understand you were found unconscious in a public toilet. Any particular reason for that?'

'You ask a lot of questions.'

'Part of the job, Blaine.' He rattled off some readings as the female paramedic joined them.

'Got that, Gary.' She recorded the data. The man who had found Blaine ran off to join his training partner.

'Sal, this is Blaine. Hasn't got a last name.' He held his hand up to his mouth and whispered loudly, 'A secret agent, I'm thinking. But maybe he'll tell us how old he is, if we ask.'

'So Blaine, I'm guessing you're about sixty-nine, right?' Sal was quick to pick up on the act.

Disarmed, Blaine released the information, which she promptly noted.

'Great. See, asking questions works.' Gary's grin was broad. 'Do you mind taking your jacket off, so I can check your blood pressure and all that?'

Blaine hesitated, remembering the reaction of the other men to the needle marks on his arms.

'I'll be quick. Will even pre-warm the stethoscope.'

'Don't they have machines for that?'

'Yep.' Gary pulled out a cuff and ripped apart the Velcro fastening pad. 'But I always do my base line BP manually.'

Sal helped ease off the jacket. Blaine wrapped his arms about his waist as a crop of goose bumps popped up across his skin. *Yeah, little chillier without that on.* At Gary's instruction, he reluctantly offered his arm, catching the glance that passed between the two medics.

More details were noted. Blaine wished Gary would hurry up with his vital signs assessment.

Gary's cheerfulness didn't seem at all diminished as he continued. 'Had a bit of needlework, Blaine?'

Blaine shrugged. 'Got some tests done.'

'Been in hospital recently?'

'Sort of.'

'Looks like they made a good pincushion out of you.' Concern broke through man's tone. Still, he was chatty and relaxed. 'Now, for that head injury.'

'I'm just going to put your jacket down here, Blaine, while Gary does his thing. I'll be back in a minute.'

Blaine winced as his head wound was cleaned.

'Probably leave a scar, you know. Any headaches or dizziness?'

Blaine shrugged then grimaced as Gary used special tape to pull together the edges of the cut.

'Sorry, but it'll feel better afterwards.'

Gary talked as he worked. Blaine knew he was trying to extract more information out of him. *Got to admit, this guy's got a talent for inquisition.* But his ears pricked up when he overheard Sal radioing in the information about him. In moments her head appeared around the side of the van.

'Hey, Gary, can I borrow you for a second?'

Gary sighed and pulled a comical expression. 'Can't wait, can she?' He put down a roll of adhesive dressing. 'Back in a minute, Blaine. You sit tight—no secret agent business for a tick.'

'Okay.' But soon Blaine heard 'POI' and low spoken details about him. *Person of interest?* He grabbed his coat and slipped away into the darkness.

'Thanks for waiting ... Blaine?'

Blaine turned and saw Gary looking after him. His heart rate snapped up a gear and he jumped up on a park bench to scale a retaining wall edging Riverwalk. Running across the road, he headed for the darkened backstreets, away from the river.

Glancing back, Blaine could see Gary watching his movements, but the man didn't give chase. Even still, he wasn't taking any chances, and ducked down several side streets to try and cover his tracks. Undoubtedly his whereabouts would be reported to the police.

Unsure of where to go, he decided to keep heading in the general direction of South Bank, though he was certainly taking the long way round. Forced to slow, he realised he was trembling all over. *I don't have time for this. Come on, body.* His stomach growled in accompaniment to his flagging, irregular steps and he couldn't seem to focus properly.

Blaine rubbed his eyes. *Is it just the darkness messing with them?* It was like they were fighting each other instead of ...

He stopped. Surely it couldn't happen that fast. Surely his body wouldn't degrade in a matter of days when the best part of three long years had been spent in arduous rehabilitation. He blinked until his vision grew clearer and desperately hoped it was just a symptom of his fatigue or the injury to his head, not his critically low levels of Ramer's Cure.

Blaine snorted at himself. *Who am I kidding?*

Before another thought could form, a whooshing louder than any noise around him rushed through his ears. Like a battery discharging, energy funnelled out of him into some unseen circuitry. Blaine tumbled onto the cold cement footpath.

Feeling like a marionette cut from its strings, he wrestled the unseen force that held him to the ground. He *had* to move. His focus went hazy then black. Any aspirations of making another day without calling his mother crashed in a pile.

Gotta call Mum. Gotta find a payphone.

Surely with the tertiary institutes around there would be one—somewhere. *Maritime Museum? Train station?* He knew there were phones in those locations, but he wasn't close enough now, especially given that every extra metre might as well be a kilometre.

Blaine rested for a while in the darkness, then rolled onto his side and pushed to his feet. He could barely stand, let alone walk properly. Gritting his teeth with determination, he shuffled along at a sluggish pace that made him feel like a sloth in slow motion. Disoriented, he wondered if he was even going in the right direction anymore. But he couldn't give up now.

To keep his mind from wandering, he started counting his steps, naming each one as a tick for hope—a reminder he was still alive. Relief flooded him as he recognised the street he was crossing. *Getting nearer to South Bank.* And then he spotted the lifeline he was seeking.

A phone booth.

'Please, Mum, please be home.'

CHAPTER 28

Blaine hobbled over to the payphone, his pace in stark contrast to the cars that whipped across an intersection at the far end of the street. The phone booth was in poor repair, with bold graffiti plastered across it, both inside and out. Pushing his hand into his pocket, he froze. Quickly he tried the pockets on his other leg. *That's right, no money.*

He fished around the seams of his pockets and managed to produce a five cent piece, but it wasn't even enough to send a text message.

'No!' Blaine hammered the cracked side of the booth with his fist. *Reverse charges call?* He felt stupid when he realised he didn't even know how. Then he remembered the five-dollar calling card he'd found. Despite the poor state of the payphone, he decided to check the credit. *Please, God, I'm stuck.*

With shaking fingers, he inserted the card. *Please, please, please.* He sighed when it registered. Yet, even though the display flashed up, it was so badly smashed the remaining credit reading was obscured beyond recognition. With no options beyond desperate hope, Blaine prayed the phone was still operational and the card would have enough credit on it to make the call. He was too exhausted to find more money and another phone.

He needed Ramer's Cure and he needed it *now.*

A dial tone hummed to life through the handset. *Hope! What was the count?* He couldn't remember, but a line of ticks ran through his mind.

He glanced upward. 'Thank you.'

Carefully he dialled his mother's number. He dared not ring the landline, given it could be monitored. Besides, if she wasn't home and it went to voicemail, he'd waste the call. He was sure his father was still away on his trip, but his mother should be waiting—somewhere.

Blaine sank to his knees with relief when the call connected and a ringtone began purring into his ear. On and on it went, so long he feared it might go to messages before his mother picked up. Hot tears welled up in his eyes and he scrubbed them off against the hood of his jacket.

Please.

Doubt grew as he waited. Even though he tried to push it aside, a voice taunted him from within, questioning everything he'd ever believed of his parents. What had been their motives for adopting him? Had they really wanted him? Was their faith in God a front? Had he tolerated their beliefs to diminish his own doubts? Were they only prepared to commit for a few years? Was that the reason behind sending him for gene therapy?

But then a greater fear clutched him.

What if Mum's not near her mobile? What if she doesn't believe it's me?

'Hello?'

A sob caught in Blaine's throat, bottling up his words.

'Hello? Who is this?'

He managed to croak, 'Mum.'

'Blaine? Is that you?'

'It's me, Mum.' His voice broke like shattered crystal. 'And I'm in lots of trouble.'

'Blaine, they said you hurt someone. They said you were hurt.'

Blaine's chest felt like it was caving in on him. He could hear tears in his mother's voice, but there was no time to savour the love so tangibly transmitted through the receiver.

He swallowed hard, afraid the phonecard credit might run out before he said what he needed to. 'No, Mum, I didn't hurt anyone, but please, I need your help. Don't ask questions, just pack up as many bags of Ramer's Cure as you can fit in a backpack and bring it to South Bank. Meet me at the ice creamery. And don't tell anybody.'

'Why? Where are you going that you need so many tablets?'

'Mum, *please.*'

'All right ... but shouldn't I call someone at ARI?'

'No! They're trying to get me back. Trying to poke and prod me for answers before they kill me outright. Just come as soon as you can, *please.*'

'I'll be there as soon as possible, hopefully within half-an-hour. Blaine, I love—'

The phone cut out before she could complete the words he craved to hear. Blaine hunched over further, forcing his knees into his chest. Pressing the end of the receiver against his forehead, he sobbed brokenly.

Anger and fear and loneliness swamped him in a tidal wave so huge he couldn't breathe. His heart stomped against his ribs in protest over the lack of oxygen. At last he took a great gasp of air, and then another, until he calmed himself down. Still, he felt like he was suffocating.

He couldn't go to the police, for they believed he was dangerous. It was possible they'd also land him right back at the institute without a backward glance. Of course, Dr Hartfield would say it was for his benefit, given he was an illegal GMO.

Then he felt a twitch.

He fumbled with the zipper of his cargo pocket, his fingers out of control. Concentrating, he forced them to pick up the clip-seal bag and held it at eye level.

Nothing.

Forgot it was empty.

Unable to stop the inevitable, he knew he'd never make it to the meeting place in time. Unless his mother was ridiculously late, she would be left standing, wondering where he was. As his temperature spiked and his vision darkened, he prayed he'd wake up.

CHAPTER 29

Sophie had just switched her mobile from silent when it lit up. The ringtone blared through the night air. She snatched at it as Jett's number flashed up. 'Hey. You're home.'

'Not yet. Had to stay back and help out the night crew for a bit. But I'm on my way to South Bank. Meet me there, pronto.'

Sophie halted as if lassoed from behind. 'You want me to go back to South Bank? I've just finished my shift at the restaurant.'

'Mrs Colton remembered you had to work, so called me about twenty minutes ago hoping I could come. She's supposed to be meeting Blaine but was stuck in traffic. Thought we might be able to get there faster to ensure he doesn't wander off, thinking she isn't coming. Even if she arrives ahead of us, I figure we might be able to help somehow.'

'Sure, Jett, I'm going now.'

'Meet me at South Bank Station. Bye.'

Jogging the rest of the way, Sophie unlocked her car and was soon pulling out of the park. The stale aroma of fried-fat on her uniform was more pungent inside the confines of the car. Winding down the window, she let fresh air flow in.

She had been reluctant to take her shift that night, but couldn't bring herself to call in unavailable without giving the boss any warning to replace her. At least it wasn't a long stint. Her dad had assured her he'd call if there was any news. She'd kept the phone in her pocket on silent throughout the evening.

South Bank. I knew it.

Now they could ask Blaine what was happening. As she drove, statements looped through her mind. Mrs Colton's warning about his health was first. Then came Dr Hartfield's insistence he might be dangerous.

'Got to trust my gut on this one.' Whispered prayers rose within her. If they didn't find Blaine in time, no one would be asking him anything, ever again.

'Want to take the Wheel for a spin?' It was a spontaneous suggestion Eddie was sure would receive a vehement 'no'.

'Love to, Dr Jonick.'

Eddie was baffled. Her enthusiastic tone didn't match the way she was professionally distancing him by using his title. *What are you up to, Mel?*

Sam had also phoned during dinner, reporting that Belinda Colton was again on the move with backpack in hand. Melissa's calm, pleased response to this information had doused Eddie's appetite. They all knew backpacks weren't Belinda Colton's style. She was leaving the house to meet Blaine. *And what was Sam expected to do about that, if anything? If only I could talk sense into this woman.*

Soon they were out in the fresh air. Theatregoers strolled from the performing arts centre, buzzing about the show they'd seen. The antics of young sweethearts tortured Eddie's heart as he rued the stupidity of coming here with a woman he now knew despised him.

He watched the huge wheel turn, hoisting one gondola after the next high into the air. Each occupant was offered a brilliant view of the inner city river vista.

Melissa turned to him. 'Shall I grab the tickets?'

Eddie was relieved she'd asked. It demonstrated she wasn't expecting much from their evening out. 'Go ahead. I got dinner, so you owe me.'

'Is that so?' Melissa shot him a daring smile.

Eddie had trouble reminding himself she was merely taking advantage of him.

They got to the wheel, only to discover the line was nearly fifty metres long.

'This could take all night.'

'Maybe we should go for a walk first, Mel. We can try again later.'

'Deal.' She nodded her agreement.

Back on the waterfront, they meandered towards Streets Beach. Stopping short, they settled onto one of the seats along the way.

'I had an interesting call from Sophie Faraday this afternoon.'

Eddie felt an internal prickling, like he'd swallowed a tub of dissecting pins, as he detected the calculating edge in her tone. He glanced at her. 'And?'

'Someone matching Blaine's description is wanted for questioning regarding the attack of a woman at South Brisbane train station.'

'I heard that report.' He shifted so he could better see her face. 'You don't seriously think he would have?'

Melissa shrugged. 'It certainly looked that way on the security footage, plus he would be desperate for money. I reminded her of that.' She paused, a sly smile teasing her lips. 'This morning I was also contacted by a police investigator interested in Blaine's whereabouts for questioning over the incident. I told them about his unpredictable behaviour and that it was probable he was involved; that he was also growing increasingly paranoid.'

Eddie, having leaned in to listen, drew back with a start. 'Why would you say that? It'll bring the entire research centre into question.'

'No.' She shook her head and eyed him with a smug expression. 'I ensured that everything I told them only discredited Ramer, not us. It's *his* treatment that has failed to produce reliable outcomes, instead, generating a monster.'

Rising to his feet, Eddie scraped his fingers across his eyes. 'So let me get this straight. You are *determined* to discredit Ramer by whatever means it takes, so that *your* profile will be elevated?'

'That's a bit harsh.' She came off the bench and wove her arm into his. The image of a serpent entwining its prey slipped into his mind. 'I'm just ensuring we've got the best possible record to guarantee continued public and financial support.'

'And because you've failed to make any significant progress in the last three and a half years, you'll destroy anything that *has* succeeded, just to build your own reputation, not to mention getting your fingers into Ramer's extraordinary achievements.'

Melissa threw away his arm and snarled. 'How *dare* you, Eddie?'

'Oh, I dare, Mel.'

Eddie watched her closely. Even in the darkness her eyes simmered with rage, confirming his suspicions. If she went down, she'd ensure *he* crashed in a spectacular blazing fireball along with her. His career as a research scientist had just ended.

So be it. I'm not up for a price like that. He decided it was time to let her know what he really thought. 'Ramer used a gutsy approach—'

She broke in before he could finish. 'In that his animal trials reported a thirty-four percent morbidity rate, but despite this he still carried on with the clinical trials?' Her face contorted in fury.

'Yet another point. He *developed* those animal models; a breakthrough that enabled him to trial therapies *no* other research group could. As for verification of his procedures, well, the proof is in the outcomes.'

'One long-term, sustainable "cure" out of seven? The others only gained transient or minor benefits and there have been two deaths since.'

Melissa's responses told Eddie she'd seen the case reports. *Underhandedly?* 'But that's one life that wouldn't have been *at all* without Ramer's willingness to take a risk. Those trial participants already had a death sentence. That's a fairly stark risk-benefit analysis.'

Melissa scoffed, but didn't argue the point.

'From what I understand, Blaine had complex mutations of multiple mitochondrial pathways and Ramer hit them all in *one* treatment. That's not just remarkable, it's unheard of! I still can't get my head around how he achieved it.' He transiently framed his head with his hands. 'Your trials haven't gone beyond tissue culture applications. Yet you mock him?'

'Pathway bypass therapy will be just as effective, given time.'

'But that's what Ramer recognised. Those kids don't *have* time!'

Melissa turned on her heel and strutted past Streets Beach. Eddie followed, though he wasn't sure why. He didn't want to continue the argument, but nearly collided with her when she came to an abrupt halt. It seemed she had completely forgotten his presence.

Then Eddie realised why.

'Is that who I think it is?' Her eyes were locked on a middle-aged woman standing near a series of food outlets. She was holding a backpack and scanning the crowd, as if looking for someone. 'Sam was right.' Melissa's lips morphed into a calculating smirk.

CHAPTER 30

Am I dreaming? Am I awake? Blaine couldn't tell.

He could see his parents sitting on the edge of his bed telling him how proud they were of him and how much they loved him. Without fail, these words had been his lullaby each night since his adoption. Some days tears of frustration or disappointment brimmed in their eyes. Other times challenging circumstances strummed harshly between them, but they would set aside any tension as best they could and say it anyway.

Then they would pray, ending each night with the same words. 'Lord, help Blaine to always remember how valuable he is.'

Valuable?

Scenes, like washed-out shadows, flickered across his mind.

What value was a kid in a chair without speech or motor control?

A precious treasure.

What value would he be if he found himself back in that place? Would his parents still want him? Would anyone want him?

As if woken from a feverish dream, Blaine felt the cloud of darkness lift and he swiped cold sweat from his forehead with the back of his hand. 'Well, God …' He grounded the heel of his palm against the cement below him and raised himself into a sitting position. '… if I'm supposedly so valuable and you're so real, you'd better work a way out of this soon or I'll be growing grass in a well-kept plot.'

The instant these words sprang from his mouth, the image of a calling card caught up in spider's web wedged in his mind. Impressions flowed like water in a running stream: a red convertible left unattended for a moment; free hot dogs; Sophie with her phone and guest gym pass; the drunk and his blanket; the truck and all the other 'coincidences' that had kept him from harm in recent days.

Blaine felt his doubt recede like a wave rolling off a beach. *God, right now I'll take all the help I can get.*

He laboured to his feet and stumbled away from the phone booth. Cars still flew past the intersection at the end of the street, but now there were people gathered on the corner. Had he been seen from a distance? Or a passing car maybe? They watched him and pointed, but it seemed no one was game to approach. Some were on mobile phones, gesturing his way. He wondered if they were calling the ambulance or police—or both.

Staggering through the darkness towards the river, he seemed to be looking through a pair of drinking glasses. He tried desperately to focus.

The reactions he received as he encountered other pedestrians— stares and queries of concern—told him a great deal about his appearance. He had no idea of the time. Had his mother waited? Was she wandering about trying to find him? Either way, he was determined to get there, even if it was the last thing he did.

Making it to the ice creamery, he collapsed onto a chair at a table along a small canal. A water dragon skittled out from under the table, its tail flicking against his ankle as it fled.

'Can I help you?'

Blaine's head pressed against his folded arms. Though his skin was cold to touch, sweat ran down his face and dripped onto the tabletop.

'Sir, do you need help? You look like you do.' The voice was an annoying mosquito in his ear. 'Sir?'

Blaine braced himself and managed to lift his head. 'I'll ... move ... soon.'

'Do you need me to call an ambulance? Should I call triple zero?' The teenage girl gasped and backed away. 'You're *that* guy.' Apparently she was familiar with the suspect profile being circulated.

Dropping his head back on his hands, it was all Blaine could do not to fall off the café chair. *What will I do if I've missed Mum?* This thought made his stomach spin like a fishing reel cast into an endless ocean.

And then he smelt it.

The aroma filled him like thirst-quenching water. Her signature perfume.

Mum!

He felt a hand on his back and practically fell towards the woman at his side as tension drained from his muscles.

'Blaine, let's get you the help you need.'

He looked up into Melissa Hartfield's face—and her cold, determined eyes.

Unable to get a park right at South Bank, Sophie found herself running from a nearby street. She dialled her brother as she covered the distance.

'Jett, has your train come in yet?'

'In five, Soph.'

'Great, I'll see you then.'

Jogging through the parklands, she debated with herself

whether to call Dr Hartfield. Apparently Blaine had told his mother not to. Yet, if he was really as sick as they claimed, perhaps it was best she did.

'Sophie?'

Uncertain if she'd heard the voice correctly, Sophie turned and scanned for a familiar face.

'Sophie.'

'Mrs Colton!' Relief was like a party popper releasing inside her. 'Did you find him? Did you get Blaine the medicine he needed?'

Blaine's mother turned away. Her shoulders shuddered, but she swiftly straightened them, as if forcing herself to remain calm. 'No.'

'Mrs Colton?' Sophie took the woman's arm and led her to a nearby bench. The night sounds of the river echoed about them, but her attention was centred wholly on Blaine's mother. Her inner explosion of triumph moments earlier fell flat, as the streamers of hope were grounded in a messy, tangled heap.

'I waited, but he didn't come. Instead that *woman* did. Dr Hartfield.'

'Dr Hartfield's here?'

Belinda nodded and her mouth warped. 'Saw her ten, maybe fifteen minutes ago ...' She looked up, eyes glassy. 'When I told her I was meeting Blaine and giving him Ramer's Cure, she said he was already back in their care and had sent her to meet me instead. Said he didn't even want to see us; that he was angry with us for deceiving him about his diagnosis.'

'That's rubbish.' But then Blaine's question over the timing of his diagnosis in relation to his adoption, crept back into Sophie's mind. It was clearly bothering him.

'Maybe it's not so farfetched, given he's been asking about it. I mean, how did she even know I'd be there if he hadn't told

182

them?' It was as if Belinda Colton had read Sophie's mind. 'Then again, there are only a handful of people who have access to the information surrounding Blaine's adoption and diagnosis—and Melissa Hartfield's one of them.' Belinda didn't say why Melissa knew this, but that was unimportant at that moment.

'You think *she* told him?'

'Probably, though I can't see how it'd be to her gain. Either way, I refused to accept it. Argued with them. *Demanded* they release Blaine to me. But she was insistent.' She stopped for a moment and stared blankly. 'And then she said his treatment has breached a legal agreement; that she'd sue us and have him permanently incarcerated if I didn't cooperate. So, I gave them Ramer's Cure—enough for two weeks. What else could I do?'

Belinda's voice had dropped, along with her shoulders. She pressed her hand against her forehead. 'He'd asked for more, but I thought if I only gave him that much, he'd have to contact us again. But ...'

'But what?'

'They claim Blaine's unsafe to be around.' She focussed on mangling a tissue between her fingers, twisting it into many pieces.

'They told me the same thing. Is it true?'

'I don't know. They said his condition was rapidly deteriorating and even Ramer's Cure was no longer helping. Apparently he also told Dr Hartfield he wanted us to remember him at his best, not his worst, because that's what we'd thought we were getting.'

Sophie sank onto the bench beside Belinda. Now *that* was something more like Blaine would say. But yet, it wasn't. He wouldn't do that without saying goodbye properly; without explaining himself in person. Though he *had* been acting strangely over the past few days. These conflicting messages felt like someone had stolen a priceless painting from her and shredded it into pieces—and then they'd done the same to her heart.

'I just don't know what to do. We ... we should have told him from the start. But Sophie, if we start that conversation, there's so much more ... Maybe he really doesn't want us anymore.' She inhaled a ragged breath and shrugged. 'And what if it's true about his treatment breaching an agreement? Dr Hartfield said it would be best to keep the authorities out of it for now. But something doesn't sit right with me. I came here to try and make sense of it.'

Blaine wouldn't break his mother's heart like that.

This thread wove itself into Sophie's mind and took hold. 'Mrs Colton, don't you think you deserve the right to speak to Blaine about this face-to-face?' She held Belinda's eyes a moment. Usually such a strong person, the woman was shattered over her son's situation. Worse, with Blaine's father still away, she was alone.

'I'll call Jett and get him to meet us ... where?'

'At the ice creamery. That's where I was waiting before. Isn't that where you young people meet most times?'

'Okay, though once ice cream is mentioned, Jett may beat us there.' She smiled as she brought up his number. 'I'm sure we'll be able to talk to Blaine and Dr Hartfield and sort this out. She couldn't have gone far, surely.'

'And Mike's due to land in Brisbane any minute now.'

Sophie put the phone to her ear and was pleased to see Mrs Colton attempt a smile. 'Hey Jett, meet us at the usual spot. Bye.'

Belinda and Sophie hurried back through South Bank. They'd not gone far before Jett caught up, puffing from his run.

'Am I pleased to see you, even in your cute high-visibility gear. Though you stink of work.' Sophie wrinkled her nose and squeezed his muscular arm.

'Ewww, girl germs. At least you won't lose me.'

She thumped his shoulder then let Jett lead the way. She hoped beyond hope they weren't too late.

CHAPTER 31

Blaine pushed Dr Hartfield away, but she had a firm grip on his wrist. Before he knew it, Dr Jonick had secured his other arm.

'I don't know why you're running, Blaine. You're out of Ramer's Cure, so soon enough you'll drop in a heap. Then we'll just cart you back and finish what we started. We're trying to protect you, remember? You're a danger to society, and yourself.'

'Mum!' Blaine shouted as loudly as he could as they dragged him away. 'Where's my Mum?'

'Oh, your mother's been and gone, Blaine. I explained about your paranoia and how you despise them for not really wanting you. I also reminded her you were being hunted by the police, but she kindly left something for you. It'll keep you going until you're sentenced. It's a bit embarrassing having a criminal for a son.'

'Is that *really* necessary, Mel? Blaine, please stop fighting so we can get someplace private and give you a dose of Ramer's Cure.'

'Keep your comments to yourself, *Eddie*.'

As they pulled him towards the car park, Blaine noticed a backpack hanging off her shoulder. Even in the semi-darkness he recognised it as his own.

Ramer's Cure. Within reach.

'The reality is, your parents don't want the strain of your care anymore, Blaine.' Melissa forced out her words as her breathing grew heavier from exertion.

'*Mel!*'

'What are you doing? Let me go!' Blaine squirmed and lunged for the backpack as they wrangled him into the car park, towards a glossy black sedan. They held him fast.

'Thankfully, due to your unique circumstances, I assured your mother we'd look after you. Especially as we now have the missing ingredient in all of this.' She laughed as she reached to grab something out of her handbag.

Blaine ran through ways to get the keyless remote from her— but when she raised her hand, that was not what she was holding.

'Melissa, wait … What are you doing?' Dr Jonick's voice had a raw edge to it.

'No. No!' Blaine fought with the little strength he had left, but it all ended with a sharp piercing of his thigh.

'Well, that was a bit of excitement. Never know what you'll see around these parts some nights.'

Sophie frowned at the girl wearing a uniform sporting a familiar food franchise logo. A crowd of people were staring off into the darkness.

'What happened?'

'There was some guy here a few minutes ago,' a man holding a toddler offered. 'I think he was a druggo or something. A couple of plain clothes cops took him off, but he was kicking and screaming all the way. I think they might've tasered him, though, because he quieted down fast.'

'What was he shouting?' Sophie glanced at Mrs Colton and

Jett, certain it was Blaine.

'Mum.' A waitress from a nearby restaurant nodded as she offered this information. 'He kept shouting "Mum." It looked like that fellow the police are after—you know, from the identity sketch they've been showing on the television.'

Sophie caught her brother's eye and they sprinted off in the direction everyone was still staring. Looking up and down, there was no sign of anyone dragging another person anywhere. It was strange.

'There!'

Jett bolted off again, leaving Sophie to canter in his wake. Mrs Colton trailed far behind.

Straining to see what her brother had spotted; Sophie only caught the shadow of some people entering a subterranean car park. Even Jett wasn't fast enough to see where they were headed.

She slowed to a walk when her phone rang. What were the chances of it being Dr Hartfield?

Sienna's number came up.

'Hi Sophie, just got your message and thought I'd give you a call.'

'Sienna! I didn't know if you still had your phone or not.'

'Police got it back for me. Screen's cracked, but it still works.'

'So you're doing okay now?' Sophie listened closely, able to hear monitors in the background. She wondered if her friend was even supposed to be using her mobile phone in the hospital.

'*Heaps* better, thanks.'

'Sienna, this is important. Do you remember if it was my friend Blaine who attacked you, or not?'

'So *not*. It was this manky-looking creep with a metal bar. Like you'd carry *that* round for fun? Memory's a bit sketchy, but someone shouted at him to stop; tried to push me out of the way. Police showed me the footage. Okay, so it seemed a bit incriminating, but

188

I know what I heard, and it wasn't a second man coming in to hurt me, as they thought. I'm guessing it was Blaine coming to help.'

'So you've spoken to the police?'

'Just before.'

'Thanks and get better quick. We'll catch up soon. Bye.'

Sophie ran after Jett, relief etching away the doubt that had built up like a gritty residue around her heart. '*That's* our Blaine.' She wanted to shout his innocence across every media network. Instead, she made a beeline for her brother who was still watching the car park entrance.

'Sophie. Jett.'

'Over here, Mrs Colton.' Jett raised his arm and waved to Belinda, who had her phone to her ear.

'They're lying, Jett.' Sophie turned around and raised her voice. 'Mrs Colton, Blaine does *not* want to cut ties with you. He was calling out "Mum". And he *didn't* attack Sienna. We need to go get him, now. We need to help Blaine.'

'Whoa, Soph.' Jett gripped her shoulders, preventing her from running into the car park. 'It may not have even been them I saw.'

Phone to her ear, Belinda held up her hand to indicate she was trying to listen. She talked for a moment longer and then hung up. 'Well, that was an interesting conversation.' Instantly she gained Sophie and Jett's full attention. 'You know that man Luke you mentioned, Sophie? Apparently he used to work with Professor Ramer. The reason he was asking questions was he'd spoken with Blaine and was concerned by some things that were said—even more so after hearing reports of that attack. So, he tracked down my contact details.'

'What else did he say?' Sophie shivered, a tumult of emotions careening through her.

'When I told him of Dr Hartfield's claims he said it's an outright

189

lie. He's going to contact Professor Ramer as soon as he can.'

'But how will that help Blaine now? His life's on the clock.' Jett threw a look back towards the car park.

'Sophie, Jett, we must involve the authorities.'

'It's not fair. We know they're lying, but he could still die.' Sophie stopped and raised her hand, her phone clasped tight against her palm. 'Wait, I've got their phone numbers. And I have an idea ...'

CHAPTER 32

Blaine woke up and squinted at the halogen lights above him. They distorted his vision so badly it made his temples pound like a subwoofer speaker at full volume. Electrode pads had been attached to him in his sleep, and the blips and beeps of a battery of monitors made a discordant rhythm nearby.

Weakness dragged at him like a sandbag. His eyes weren't just tired; he was so fatigued he couldn't make them focus. His head felt like he had been held under water too long. He tried to pinch his fingertips together and it took every scrap of concentration to achieve this simple goal.

He was regressing—fast.

A door opened nearby and Blaine immediately recognised his visitor's gait.

Dr Hartfield.

'Blaine, pleased you've come to. Now, I trust you're listening well.'

Blaine grunted an acknowledgement. He wondered if he could even speak.

'I have a proposition.' She paused, as if expecting another response, but Blaine remained silent. 'I'll give you your doses of Ramer's Cure and you'll do exactly as I ask.' She held up two tablets as evidence, and then put them on a small tray near his bed. 'We need **you, Blaine. You** can help a generation of Mitochondrial Disease sufferers, but it will take a great deal of sacrifice. I can't do it without your cooperation. I'll need you to sign a form for me and date it your birthday, this year. You'll be an adult within weeks. It will ensure we have the best chance of achieving similar results for other sufferers. The deal is, I won't report you to the regulating body.'

'Danger?' It was so hard to speak.

'I'm now convinced, Blaine, that whatever vector Professor Ramer used, it's not transmissible. But you are still illegal. That carries with it ramifications and responsibilities.'

She waited. Again, he wondered why.

'Will you sign it? I noticed your breathing is getting increasingly laboured. You may not last long if you don't get some of that Cure. There are two tablets right here on the tray. I'll leave them with you. You just need to sign and then I'll help you.' She positioned the call button within his slackened grip. 'Use it when you've made up your mind.'

Blaine felt, more than saw her retreat to the exit. He couldn't move more than a finger, and she knew it.

'I'll let you think about it. I'm sure you'll come to the right decision.'

His parents had always reminded him of how special he was and how his life had a purpose beyond what he imagined. Maybe this was for the best. Maybe this was his value; his destiny. To give up his life, so that others might live.

'Melissa, you can't do this. It's wrong. Give him the Cure.'

She ignored Eddie's drawn face and messy hair as she left Blaine's room. 'You helped me get him into the car.'

Eddie dogged her along the corridor. 'Yeah, I'm an idiot, aren't I?'

She studied him a moment and offered a measured smile. 'Actually, I believe you're a smart man protecting his interests; that being your future in the scientific profession.' Folding her arms, she leaned against the wall. 'I don't believe you were thinking clearly earlier tonight. I'll give you a chance to straighten your head and we can start over.'

'Mel, I'm giving him the meds and taking him home. I thought at least you'd do *that* much when you brought him back here, *before* you made him unconscious.'

'Eddie ...' She drummed her fingers against her arm and arched her brow. 'It's too late for that. If I go down for this, so do you—and if we don't do this, we'll go down anyway.'

'*We?*' Eddie frowned, as if trying to decipher her exact meaning, but she was in no mood to enlighten him. 'First thing we need to do is get him to a more secure site.' She studied an invisible point before her. 'I don't think his parents will be satisfied with my explanation for long.'

'And so they shouldn't be.' Eddie grabbed her arm and gave her a slight shake. 'I've worked out why you're doing this. It's AXON Corp. isn't it? If you don't produce results, they're about to take back their four million dollar grant. True?'

Melissa felt her face flinch as a nervous pulse jerked next to her eye.

'True!'

She hated that she'd given herself away. But he'd only guessed the half of it.

'Ego and money. You lied to me and used me, and you lied to Blaine and his family.' Eddie shook his head. 'It's *not* worth it.'

She shrugged him off and tossed her head. '*Says you*, scientist underachiever of the decade.'

Maybe I overstepped a line there. She caught the sudden clench of his jaw and decided not to push it. He couldn't seriously relocate Blaine without her notice. She'd already called security and had his access to the observation room revoked. 'Tomorrow, I want profiles on those pills. Goodnight, Eddie. I'll take it from here.'

Eddie folded his arms and moved to block her path. 'You stay, Mel, I stay. Let's call it the perfect end to the perfect date.'

Swallowing, Melissa tried to cover her unease with another toss of her head. Eddie was becoming unpredictable. She went straight to her office and locked the door behind her. The bags of Ramer's Cure were locked in with her. She'd made sure of that, just in case Eddie decided to be a hero. He'd been given enough to test and no more.

Realising she'd missed a call from a restricted number, Melissa checked her voicemail messages. Already jumpy, she felt queasy when Professor Ramer's familiar voice sounded in her ear, requesting an urgent appointment.

'Diplomatic as always, but no, Professor, you're *not* winning this time.'

But am I?

Time ticked by. Thoughts rammed through her head like a free-swinging wrecking ball. *Why's he contacting me now, after all this time? Could he possibly know about Blaine?*

Despite her attempts to sleep in her darkened room, Melissa couldn't get comfortable on her reclined office chair. She took off her jacket to use as a pillow, but it didn't help. With no waist band on her dress to clip her swipe card onto, she placed it on her desk within arm's reach. No way would she let *that* out of her sight.

Light from the corridor peered under the door. Occasionally she saw Eddie's shadow pass by. Sometimes his familiar stride would pause outside her office, other times he was clearly pacing. Once he even thumped on the one-way glass between her office and the lab, making her start with a violence that nearly toppled her off the chair.

Convinced her climbing heartrate would never let her rest, Melissa dozed off into a fitful sleep with strange dreams about creatures that were part-rat, part-human.

CHAPTER 33

Melissa nearly tumbled off her chair when the door handle turned. In seconds, the door started to move. At the same instant, her phone sprang to life. Jumping again, her breath lodged in her throat as she checked the display of her phone. It was a private number.

She decided not to answer the call and let it go to voicemail. Shivering, she reached for her jacket as a cleaner stepped through the door and then backed swiftly out, apologising for the intrusion. Melissa called after him, but he was gone. Her phone began ringing again. *Another restricted number?*

With shaking hands, she took the call, expecting it to be Professor Ramer. 'Hello.'

'Dr Melissa Hartfield?'

'Yes ...?'

'This is Detective Boyd from the Queensland Police. We believe you have a young man by the name of Blaine Colton in your care. And we have a warrant for his arrest.'

Melissa glanced up to find Eddie standing opposite her desk. His eyes were dark and his jaw set. Arms folded, he had a piece of paper in his hand.

'I'm sorry, it's late. Can I call you back?'

'Dr Hartfield, it's three o'clock in the morning. Can you please confirm whether or not you have Blaine Colton in your custody?'

Swallowing hard, Melissa tried to force herself to remain calm. But a flush of heat spread across her face. It was accompanied by an ice-cold gush through her stomach. 'I'm sorry, Detective, but Blaine is under observation at the institute I work for. He is unstable and until his health condition is managed, we are unable to transport him anywhere. Goodbye.' She ended the call.

Eddie shook his head and uncrossed his arms. Without breaking eye contact, he spun the paper at her like a rectangular frisbee. 'There's your profile. And *thanks* for changing my card access.'

The angle of his jaw told Melissa she'd pushed it too far. She tensed, as if he might strike her. 'I had to take precautions.' She chose to ignore his snort.

Taking the report, Melissa scanned the primary ingredients. There appeared to be only one compound of note. 'Closest match seems to be some sort of synthetic compound. Similar properties to an artificial sweetener? You've obviously done it wrong.'

'Or Mrs Colton didn't actually *give* you Ramer's Cure, just a placebo.' He shrugged. 'Dunno. I put it through the analyser, that's what came out. Not really a chemist.'

Balling up the page, Melissa pelted the wad at Eddie and jumped up from her chair. 'No! Not this close, only to fail. The Professor *owes* me this. If his guinea pig keels over on us now, I'll hunt Ramer down and *make* him talk.'

'I thought you mostly knew what Professor Ramer did? Could it be those reports you were so occupied with last month were *failed* milestones? Sweet talk not working for you, Mel? Maybe you could take some Ramer's Cure to sweeten you up. Then again, maybe our dear Mrs Colton isn't such a loving mummy after all and wanted to dispose of her son in a rapid fashion. Or *maybe* she realised you were just a pretender with a fudged-up research history trying to claw your way to recognition through her child, and thought it would be amusing to see you declare the amazing cure to be artificial sweetener.'

His glare fell away. Melissa forced herself to breathe. He seemed fixated by something on her desk. She followed his line of sight, understanding milliseconds too late.

Eddie snatched up her access card and let it dangle from his fingers. 'How careless, Mel.'

With a cry of rage, she lunged across her desk and took a swipe at him. As she fell hard against the desktop, her phone rang again. A restricted number, just as before.

'You'd better answer that. And B-T-W, I've called the police.'

She wanted to rip the smirk off Eddie's face and shove it in a biohazard bag. Instead, she picked up the phone and took the call. 'Dr Hartfield speaking.'

'Dr Hartfield, this is Detective Boyd. If you continue to obstruct the course of justice, we'll be forced to place charges against you.'

'Ah ...' Melissa dropped back onto her chair. 'What ... what are the charges against Blaine? If this is to do with the South Brisbane incident—'

'No.'

She stopped. 'It's not?'

She felt faint as she listened to multiple allegations. Despite her fabricated claims to fool his family and friends, she could not reconcile such violence with an ill boy like Blaine. But they had two separate witnesses who had accurately identified him and provided corroborating accounts of the incident. She swallowed again, but there was no saliva left in her mouth.

'I ... I understand those are very serious allegations, but I'm—'

'*Give* him the medication and *take* him there.' Eddie's voice sizzled through the air like a high frequency whistle.

Rising from her chair, she turned her back on him and tried to block out his insistent demands. 'I'm sorry, Detective, but it's not possible, we—'

She stopped. Pressing the phone to her chest, she strained her ears toward the door. 'What's that alarm?'

Eddie's head snapped around and he set off at a bolt.

Blaine. Melissa began running after him. 'I'm sorry, Detective. I've got to go.' He continued to talk, but Melissa shoved the phone into her pocket.

CHAPTER 34

Melissa pushed through the door behind Eddie. 'His breathing's shutting down. Get a resuscitation mask and hook him up to oxygen, or something. Tell me what he needs.'

'Eddie, we don't know what—'

'Shut up, Melissa! And here's your stupid card.' He tossed it at her and gave Blaine two ventilation breaths.

'Two people in the sample group died post-therapy.'

Eddie's head came up, his eyes dark with anger. 'And four died *awaiting* gene therapy. Quit your fear-mongering, Mel, and call Carl— or *someone* from the hospital. He's not far off cardiac arrest. How are you going to "fix" him then without a heart-lung machine? He can't exactly take his pills now, can he?' He gave another two breaths.

She clenched her jaw as she prepared the oxygen line. After attaching a resuscitation mask to the tubing, she signalled for Eddie to stop. Hot tears ran down her nose as she bent to position the mask over Blaine's mouth and nose. Fear and fury thrashed within her as she turned on the flow to the required rate.

Slowly Blaine's breathing stabilised and his heart rate improved, but Eddie was quite right. Because of the boy's condition, his body couldn't use the oxygen efficiently. His vital signs were deteriorating. And what excuse would she have for a dead young man in her institute, in *her* purpose-built observation unit?

'We've got to dump him, Eddie.'

'What?' Eddie wheeled about to face her. 'There is *no way* I'm letting you dump Blaine off somewhere.'

'We've got enough samples to do a substantial amount of analysis and continue the research. It wouldn't be our problem then, Eddie. We'll just say he escaped after we tried to help him and there was nothing more we could do.'

'You've done enough damage already. I should have stopped you sooner.'

Eddie's words drifted through her mind, uncomprehended. Melissa felt increasingly self-assured the more she talked. 'It's the only way. If he dies here, it's our problem—and a problem that's not going away. But if he's gone and all the security footage has been taken care of, well ...?'

She started disconnecting electrodes. Eddie reached across Blaine and wrestled with her, holding her hands away so she couldn't touch the oxygen mask.

'Melissa!' His voice boomed through her head. 'You've just admitted having custody of him to a police detective. Not only that, you've claimed him to be unwell and unstable. How do you think you'll be able to convince them of such a miraculous recovery that you were unable to keep him contained? I *won't* let you do this to Blaine. Not anymore.'

She stared at him. Her breathing grew ragged as the reality of the impossible situation she'd created squeezed the sense from her mind. A stream of sirens screamed from the nearby hospital, the sounds of a major emergency in direct contrast to the piercing silence strung between them in that moment. The only noise was the steady beeping of a monitor.

Soon Eddie found his voice. 'You did a medical degree, Mel. You might have done biomed in your higher degrees, but you're a medical researcher. A doctor. You trained to *preserve* life.'

'And promote it through research.' Something in her snapped. 'And Ramer has stolen that opportunity from me.'

She ripped her hands away so hard that Eddie's grip slipped. Lunging at the monitors, she threw them over, smashing them onto the floor in a domino-like series of clatters. As she turned over the final machine, the oxygen gear tore away from Blaine and flew across the room.

Eddie looked from her to Blaine. The instruments were going berserk. Melissa's unrestrained hair fell over her face, matching the frenzy of her state. As if she wasn't even there cursing and ranting, he began rescue breaths once again.

'You can't do that forever. It won't help anyway. Nature has determined he should die. You can't stop it.'

He ignored her.

Melissa reached out to shove Eddie's shoulder. 'I said, we need to *dump* him.'

Eddie stopped to glare. 'Call the hospital. Get them to send someone across. *Now!*' He then returned to breathing on Blaine's behalf.

Air came from her nostrils in heavy snorts. She was prepared to do *anything* to have her way. She pulled her phone from the pocket of her jacket, ready to hurl it at Eddie. As she drew back her hand, her heart lunged to her toes.

She'd not hung up the call from the police.

Noooooo… Her wail was so high-pitched it was almost silent.

Quickly she stabbed 'end call' with her finger. 'Eddie, we need to run!'

Still he bent over the boy.

Melissa swiped her card and wrenched open the door. From the opposite direction she could see a dozen police officers with weapons drawn. They reached the external door to the anteroom and pulled at it. The vibrations shuddered through the walls.

'Open the door or we'll batter it down!'

Frozen, Melissa couldn't go forward or back. She remained glued to the internal door, scarcely aware as Eddie moved past her to open the external access.

The police rushed in and tackled them both to the floor.

'Help the boy.' Eddie's voice squeezed out, despite the strong men restraining him.

Once the police had them on the linoleum in handcuffs, they were followed by paramedics, the security guard, Sam, and one other man. Melissa could see only this man's shoes. She strained to twist her head. She knew she could convince the detective; she just needed a chance. But the man had a face she recognised. 'Professor Ramer!'

He stood at the bed while the paramedics assessed Blaine's vital signs. Glancing down, he caught her eye and shook his head. 'Did you *really* think you'd get away with this, Melissa?' His look was much like a father might offer a disobedient child. 'And was it worth it?' He caught sight of the tray where she had left the tablets of Ramer's Cure.

Melissa hadn't thought to smash those too.

'Re-attach the oxygen then dissolve those tablets in normal saline. We need to filter sterilise the solution and administer the dose i.v.—as quickly as possible.'

'It's only some sort of synthetic sweetener.'

Melissa wanted to kick Eddie. *Let the brat die and finish Ramer's flop.* He'd ruined her life. But Professor Ramer's chuckle rumbled into her thoughts.

'Not quite, Edward.' He ensured he had their attention. 'It's a compound the body cannot synthesise or, under normal conditions, utilise. Essentially it's inert, except to cells in which the defective DNA has been successfully exchanged. The therapy embedded sequences that, once integrated along with the functional DNA, enable the compound to be taken up by the cell to induce a cascade of rescue processes. If we're lucky it will take effect in time. If not ...' His face sobered. 'Seems you didn't quite grasp the science, Melissa.'

'Where's Detective Boyd?' Melissa mumbled this into the floor, more so out of contempt than any real interest in gaining an introduction. The police officers hauled her and Eddie out of the room, down to the waiting vehicle.

Two adolescents were standing with the Coltons near the building's exit. One of them she recognised as Sophie, Blaine's friend. The other she didn't know.

'*There's* your Detective Boyd.' They turned her slightly towards the group.

'That kid?'

'Yeah, this "kid",' the young man's voice chased after her as she was eased into a police car, 'aka Jett, Blaine's other best friend. Best prank call I ever made—and the cops at the local station thought so, too, when we let them in on it. Soph recorded every second of it, right in front of them.'

CHAPTER 35

Blaine opened his eyes and looked around. He was in a stainless-steel chamber. At least, it felt like it. Every surface reflected back his image in a distorted fashion, and it smelled so clean the air felt cold as it entered his lungs.

He was held in place by some large, padded braces. He tried to move his head, but it was also secured with an elasticised padded strap. There were wires coming off him everywhere.

'Blaine, welcome back.'

He recognised the voice but couldn't place it.

'Don't worry. You're at the facility where I now work.'

'Professor Ramer?' Blaine tried this name, figuring it to be the most logical of the options running through his mind. His articulation didn't seem to be quite as controlled as in his recent past, and he stumbled over multiple syllables.

'Yes, Blaine.'

The Professor stood near enough to be in Blaine's field of view. He was wearing a military uniform.

'I realise this is not protocol. However, given the extraordinary life-and-death circumstances, I was given permission by the appropriate agencies to intervene, so I brought you here for the finest care. I also wanted to monitor you fully until you were stable and on the way to recovery.'

'Where are we?'

Ramer smiled. 'I could tell you but then I'd have to kill you. And that would defeat the purpose of saving you, wouldn't it?' The smile broadened and he winked. 'Everything I do now is for the military. I can't be traceable whilst acting in this role.'

'But how did I get here? And how long have I been here?'

A great sigh lifted Professor Ramer's chest. He expelled it from his lungs in a long exhalation. 'Do you remember Drs Hartfield and Jonick taking you back to ARI from South Bank? That was over a week ago.'

Blaine tried to nod, but it was hard with the head gear.

'Here, let me help.' Ramer leaned over and released him from the protective restraints.

Blaine eased to a sitting position and let his body acclimatise to this change. *Whoa, major head spin.* He closed his eyes and waited for the room to stop feeling like a merry-go-round. Blinking several times, he said, 'I remember, but after that it's all messed up. Like a weird dream.'

'She nearly killed you by her neglect and selfish ambition. You were on the brink of cardiac arrest when the police intervened.'

'Oh.' Blaine swallowed hard. 'Is there ... damage?' Sophie's face darted through his mind.

'Some, Blaine, I'm afraid. But probably not so much that you'll notice it in time—although there will always be an elevated risk, given your background. And, of course, you'll need more rehab. You suffered many seizures, some quite prolonged.'

'I know.' He offered a wry smile. 'And what are you going to do about the regulating body?'

Ramer frowned and drew up a chair on castors from a

nearby bench. He sat down, putting his eyes level with Blaine's. 'Under special consideration of my unique position, I'm still head of the collaborative research group and co-contact, so am in communication with all appropriate personnel, regulating authorities and committee heads. The "regulating body" you refenced, separate to these matters, recently made contact post-inspection after witnessing an odd conversation between your mother and Melissa Hartfield—about you. When Luke rang me on an old number I rarely use and detailed Melissa's claims, along with the conversations he'd had with you and your mother, I grew increasingly concerned.'

'Dr Hartfield said the treatment wasn't approved, that I was potentially infectious, and that you changed the therapy for me.'

The Professor snorted. 'Vixen. Yes, it was an aggressive delivery system, but it had to be. And yes, it was modified in your case—because it was a custom-made therapy to address the specific mutations that caused each study participant's condition. Everything was not only fully-documented from our end, and conducted according to the agreed protocols at your end by the PI, but everything fell within the parameters submitted for approval. That was the point of the technology. That's why only people with certain types of Mitochondrial Disease were accepted into the study—and only those on borrowed time, with no options left.'

'So was it legal?'

'Most certainly! Melissa didn't know what it was and was desperate to find out for her gain. What she didn't know, she fabricated to save face. The details of the procedure are restricted by stringent confidentiality agreements that now include the military. They were so impressed by the technology they enlisted my services.'

'And what was it exactly?'

207

A chuckle rang from deep in Professor Ramer's throat. 'That, young Blaine, is another one of those things I'd have to kill you right after I told you. You've been provided all necessary information via the PI. However, what I can reiterate is the treatment was multi-modal and involved both nuclear and mitochondrial rescue mechanisms.'

'So I'm not carrying some exotic disease?'

Ramer smiled and shook his head. 'As you may remember from the information package, attenuated viruses and virus-like delivery particles were used, along with other mechanisms, to facilitate full-body therapy and target key organs. And it worked. The downside was the strong inflammatory response this elicited. This is why you were kept under constant medical surveillance for several months post-therapy. But no, you're not infectious.'

Blaine sighed, relief rolling over him like a storm cloud making way for the sun. 'So why do I have to keep taking Ramer's Cure?'

The Professor folded his arms and took another deep breath. 'I did re-explain this during that special meeting with you and your parents, but when developing the therapy, we believed using chemical regulation was the best way to control the gene expression and related processes introduced through your therapy. It's more complicated than I can detail, but by not taking Ramer's Cure you essentially shut down the rescue mechanisms, depriving your system of the necessary energy required to function. Dually, this failure enables metabolic by-products to rapidly build up to a harmful level.'

'So, the fevers I have to live with forever?'

Ramer's face grew serious. 'About that. Initially we thought perhaps a mild stroke or severe convulsive episode had damaged your hypothalamus or cerebral blood flow, or such. Another thought was maybe one of the mutations generating toxic metabolites had not been effectively silenced—but your sequencing results don't support this theory.'

Blaine considered this for a moment. 'That's why my genome was re-sequenced after the twenty-seven month consult?'

'Correct. Consequential analysis, which is still ongoing, suggests an introduced fragment may have incorporated randomly and turned off a repressor gene. A lack of regulation may cause excess by-product to build up in your system and cause a fever spike. If unmanaged, it may be a reasonable explanation for your seizures. *If* this is the issue, perhaps sleep enables your body to metabolise *some* of this, but even Ramer's Cure will only partially control your symptoms. At least, that's what we *think* may be the cause—but that too is unconfirmed.'

Blaine fell silent. He turned the facts over in his mind, grasping the full impact.

Forever.

That's how long he needed Ramer's Cure.

'So I've still got defective genes?'

Ramer nodded. 'I'm afraid so. The therapy was intended to offset the balance of defective genes to functional ones, offering sustained benefits and quality of life. You've more than exceeded our expectations, but it's not perfect.'

'Why, then, did you only produce five years supply of Ramer's Cure?'

The Professor smiled. 'Because I'd challenged myself that time to develop a more targeted therapy to enable your body to self-regulate the integrated genetic segments.'

'And have you developed that remedy?'

The Professor slowly shook his head. 'We're close, Blaine. In fact, there are several promising options that could bypass some of the difficulties we encountered with your trial. But the interactions are far more complicated than you could imagine. Even your last bank of tests has alerted us to something else.'

Blaine's stomached clenched. 'Something bad?'

He shrugged. 'Not sure. Time will tell, and further analysis. The PI will keep you informed, that is, depending on what agreement the committee comes back with after considering this rather unique situation. The other difficulty is I've had to prioritise other projects. I work for the military, remember? They have a fairly defined "to do" list.'

Ramer grinned, but Blaine didn't return the smile.

'That project is in progress ... steadily, but I'd like to establish a dedicated team to fast-track it.' He paused and held Blaine's gaze. 'Even then, you'd risk further treatment being ineffective, worsening the condition, or creating a new problem.'

'But I'll still get told when you've worked something out?'

Ramer's expression softened and the lines of his brow smoothed. 'Of course, Blaine. It would be available through the appropriate channels—maybe even ARI's clinical trials unit, now that Melissa's not muddying the water.'

'So, Professor, am I a legal GMO?'

'Absolutely, young man.'

CHAPTER 36

'Happy eighteenth birthday, Blaine. How about a gift?'

Blaine looked up as he secured the buttons of a borrowed shirt. His fingers still lacked some of the dexterity he had developed over his years of intensive physiotherapy. His physical abilities were also not quite what they'd been, but apparently things were looking good for his continued improvement.

'Sounds great, Professor.'

Ramer smiled. 'Shall we get you saddled up for a helicopter ride, then? Your parents are awaiting you at a military base en route. They refused to stay at home, insisting they be as near as possible, even if they couldn't actually be with you. Your father has now fully investigated the hygiene practices of the facility, and I believe the defence force will feel all the more "sanitised" for his visit.' He paused, a twinkle in his eye. 'Perhaps we should send him to visit Melissa. Might help clean up her act.'

Blaine's grin warped as he realised how much his doubt, aided by Melissa Hartfield's lies, had tainted his view of his parents. They were his allies, not conspiring enemies. 'What's going to happen to her and Dr Jonick?'

'Melissa is defiant to this day, maintaining she's done nothing wrong. She was an excellent student and researcher, but grew far too ambitious for her own good.' The Professor's usually steady eye grew distant. 'A real shame.'

'And Dr Jonick?'

'Edward is cooperating fully with the police and has been released on bail.'

'They let him out?' *Justice fail.*

Professor Ramer nodded. 'In a way it's fitting, given he was trying to help you when the police burst in on them.'

'He was? Why, after bringing me back to ARI with Dr Hartfield?'

Again Professor Ramer's response seemed weighted. 'Many reasons, some of which only he could say. But I ... I can't help feeling somewhat responsible, in part.'

This made no sense to Blaine. 'You weren't even there. How could it be your fault?'

'Exactly, Blaine. I wasn't there. Melissa never would have gotten away with it, if I were.' He sighed. 'But I can't change it now and I did promise you a helicopter ride.'

'When can we go?' Blaine couldn't stem the excitement that bubbled up within him.

Professor Ramer's answer was to open the door and gesture for Blaine to pass through it. 'We'll be there by lunch.'

Even when they'd landed, the constant thudding of the helicopter blades echoed in Blaine's ears. He hadn't been able to wipe the smile off his face the entire journey. Of all career choices, he'd always believed a pilot would be one of the most liberating. Perhaps it was the sense of freedom he'd always imagined flying would unleash. Until his gene therapy it was merely an imagined, unattainable dream. Yes, maybe he should enquire—except for the fact he hated sitting still for long periods.

As they scuttled across the helipad, heads down and shoulders hunched against the air beating over them, a tingle of excitement sparked through him. Glancing up, the tingle converted to a fully charged bolt as he spied his parents waiting for him near the landing site.

'Blaine!'

He broke away from Professor Ramer and ran to them. Falling into their arms, he let their words, tears, kisses and love wash over him like a soothing balm.

'Happy birthday, darling. We've missed you dreadfully.'

'We're so sorry for doubting you, Blaine, and sorry we didn't tell you your diagnosis was made after your adoption. We should have come right away when Dr Hartfield claimed things weren't right.'

When everyone had said their piece, at least for the moment, Blaine drew back a little and glanced beyond his parents. 'No one else with you?'

He caught their look and the silent smile that passed between them. A warm flush crept up his neck.

His dad answered the unspoken question. 'No, son, Sophie's not here.'

'She wouldn't have been allowed, anyway.'

Blaine looked to Professor Ramer and nodded. 'Oh.'

'But, I'm on my way to catch up with Luke in Brisbane's CBD and thank him for his part in rescuing you from Melissa's scheme. You don't suppose Sophie would mind meeting you at South Bank or the like?'

Blaine felt a grin break across his mouth. He tried hiding it for a moment, then gave up.

'We brought you some clean clothes.' His mother offered.

'And here's your mobile phone and wallet. They were found amongst Melissa's things.' Ramer took the items from his jacket and offered them. 'I forgot to pass them back earlier. Couldn't help but notice your phone's wallpaper when it was checked for any interference by my seditious protégé.'

Heat concentrated into Blaine's cheeks. He ducked his head as he took them from Professor Ramer. He was about to put the phone in his pocket when the Professor tutted at him.

'Blaine, you need to learn how to impress a girl properly. First off, you'd best give her time to get ready. Phone's charged. Call her. We'll be flying in soon.'

Blaine looked to see if he was serious. The Professor nodded. His parents also grinned their approval. 'Thank you, Professor Ramer—for everything.'

Soon it was all arranged. Blaine took the bag of clothes, changed, and then hugged his parents goodbye before they headed on home.

He and Professor Ramer were then on their way. At first butterflies tickled his stomach, but soon they turned into flapping Pterodactyls. Unable to settle his nerves, Blaine rested his head back against the seat and closed his eyes for the duration of the trip.

It was mid-afternoon when they reached the city. The helicopter landed at a heliport Blaine never knew existed. He and Professor Ramer caught a CityCat across the river and walked to the ice creamery, the prearranged meeting place with Sophie. He sensed the Professor felt responsible for ensuring he was delivered safely.

'You like ice cream, I take it?'

Blaine smiled. 'We usually meet here because Jett, Sophie's twin brother, is obsessed with the stuff.'

'They're a bright pair. Essentially they facilitated the rescue. Thanks to Luke and the investigators, I just happened to be on my way when the police alert came through.'

Professor Ramer's words echoed unheard as Blaine stalled. There she was, sitting on a café chair, scanning the crowd for him. Sophie wore a pair of white denim jeans, a pretty knitted top, and a softly toned scarf that brought out the green in her eyes. *Prof was right. I did need to give her time to dress.*

And then she saw him.

'Blaine!'

Before he could count to five, she had her arms wrapped around his neck. 'Thanks for coming, Soph.' It required every scrap of self-possession to not kiss her lipstick-pink mouth. Even as she relaxed her hold and turned to the Professor, Blaine kept one arm around her.

'Hi, Professor Ramer. Thanks for looking after him so well.'

'It was a pleasure tending your young man, Sophie.'

Sophie flushed and dropped her gaze. 'Bet he was a pain some days. Blaine's like that.'

'Gee, *thanks*.' Blaine squeezed her lightly. As if reminded of his nearness, she turned towards him and looked up into his face.

'Seriously, we're so relieved you're okay. All those tubes and machines really scared me when they wheeled you out of that place.'

'I hardly remember a thing.' He grinned as Sophie wrinkled her nose and pushed against him.

'Probably a good thing. Thank goodness it's over and you're now fine. It's about time you got to enjoy your future.'

Blaine's fresh understanding of his condition tumbled back into his mind. He pulled away and pressed his hand against his forehead. 'Oh ... man. I'm sorry, Sophie. I wanted to see you so bad I didn't even think.'

She planted her hands on her hips. 'What are you talking about?'

With a glance at Professor Ramer, Blaine burrowed his fists into the pockets of his jeans. 'Sophie, I'm *not* fine. It's not over. It was stupid and selfish of me to have asked you to do this.'

'I'm not scared of you, Blaine Colton.'

'Well, you should be. I carry defective DNA—a heritable condition. I'm no good for anyone.'

'I don't care that your DNA's dodgy. You're the nicest guy I know.'

'As a chair warmer? What about when my nappy needs changing?' He snorted contemptuously. 'You're stuck on New Year's and have forgotten what it was like before.'

Sophie flinched as his words cut her, making Blaine feel like a heartless weasel. Her face whitened and he nearly missed the faint quiver that snuck across her mouth.

'It doesn't matter, Blaine.'

'Actually ...'

They turned as Professor Ramer spoke.

'He's right, Sophie. The procedure was experimental. We don't know what might happen in the coming years. Although the patches have integrated and seem to be working, there's no guarantee Blaine's condition won't deteriorate. And it doesn't just affect his mitochondrial DNA. Even though mitochondrial DNA is maternally inherited, the nuclear defects could be passed onto his children—*if* that eventuates sometime in the future.'

Children? Blaine felt heat surge through his body and flash across his face. He glanced at Sophie. When their eyes connected, she too blushed.

'I ... I, ah, wasn't exactly thinking *that* far ...' It was then he realised, if they were talking about the future long-term, this was a valid consideration.

'There are currently investigations into such matters, but even for day-to-day life, if Blaine takes Ramer's Cure he's fine; without it ...' Professor Ramer shrugged. 'Plus there are some other issues that have been created by the therapy and his recent health crisis.'

These words struck Blaine hard and he buried his hands even deeper into his pockets. Sophie mightn't have been afraid of his condition, but he was. He could feel her eyes on him, but kept his gaze fixed on the pavement.

'So there's no hope for us?'

He glanced up. 'Not really.'

The Professor cleared his throat. 'I never said there wasn't hope. I wouldn't do what I do otherwise. Better solutions might be only a number of years away.'

Blaine straightened as fragile optimism framed a brighter future. *Could that be another tick for hope?*

'Or decades—or never.' Professor Ramer shrugged as Blaine's hope splintered into shards. 'That's always the risk.'

'And you don't think I'm worth the risk?'

'Worth it?' A wry smile twisted Blaine's mouth. 'Sophie, I'd swim to New Zealand and back to have three minutes with you. Jett might even come along for the ice cream.'

'You can hardly swim two laps of a pool.' Her eyes remained serious, despite the teasing in her tone. 'But in reality ...?'

Blaine looked into her questioning green eyes. There was an uncertainty in their depths that made him want to be done with it and kiss her as if nothing else mattered.

But it did. Even with Professor Ramer's hint of possibilities.

He shook the thought out of his head. 'In reality, my body could give up and you'd be left to deal with that, Sophie. It wouldn't be fair to you.'

'But what if it doesn't give up? Because of fear, we'd miss out on sharing your best years.'

She was far too convincing and Blaine felt his carefully-reasoned arguments crumble. She was looking at him, as if waiting for him to do something—say something—to change his mind.

Blaine shook his head. 'It wouldn't be fair.' But like a fish to a lure, he moved nearer. 'It's my problem, and shouldn't be yours.'

Sophie held his gaze. Blaine watched as pain displaced the uncertainty in her eyes. He wanted to gather her to him and make that pain stop, but he couldn't. It was the reality of his condition.

'Blaine, I respect you for telling me how you feel and I understand why, but if you don't mind, I'm going to pretend that for just one day it *doesn't* matter.'

A flutter whipped through Blaine's stomach as she slipped her hand into his.

'For just *one* day I'm going to have another New Year's Day, only this time Jett's not going to bring us ice cream.'

Her smile split through the shadow of her sadness, and he couldn't help but return it. An electric charge tingled across the insides his ribs. The only thing he could liken it to was that moment on a rollercoaster, at the top of the first hill, before the cars were released. All that potential kinetic energy and anticipation, paused against gravity, awaiting that instant drop. 'All right, then.'

Definitely another tick for hope.

Slipping his arm around her shoulders, he flashed Professor Ramer a grin and walked off for a day of impossibilities.

After all, he would only turn eighteen once.

ACKNOWLEDGEMENTS

I would like to thank Anne Hamilton and Omega Writers Inc., sponsors of the CALEB Award, for seeing potential in the unpublished *Integrate* manuscript and, in conjunction with Rochelle Stephens and the Wombat Rhiza Press team, making this novel a reality.

To my family, writing compatriots and Quirky Quills, science geek associates and friends, thank you for your enthusiastic encouragement, chats of tea (or coffee on big days), humour and sharing the heady ride from initial drafts, through editing hysteria (thank you Nola Passmore!), to final print. I am blessed to have you in my world.

Particular gratitude to my husband, Jeff, and daughter, Keziah, for indulging my writing obsession and overlooking too many weird-hour stints where 'I've just got to check/edit/read a few more sections'. Love you both.

And to the Master Author, my greatest inspiration of all, may this story be a reminder of the value You place on each of us.

ABOUT THE AUTHOR
ADELE JONES

Australian author, Adele Jones, writes young adult fringe, science-fantasy and near-science fiction that explores the underbelly of bioethics and confronting teen issues, including disability, self-worth, loss, domestic conflict, and more.

She also writes historical fiction, poetry, inspirational non-fiction and short fictional works, with themes of social justice, humanity, faith, natural beauty and meaning in life's journey. Adele's first YA novel *Integrate* (book one of the Blaine Colton Trilogy) was awarded the 2013 CALEB Prize for unpublished manuscript. As a speaker she seeks to present a practical and encouraging message by drawing on themes from her writing.

To find out more visit www.adelejonesauthor.com